ECLECTICA

(Eclectic: selecting from various styles, ideas or sources. (Collins Dictionary)

The Collected Poems
of
Brian Jackson

For Alona — a most sincere and faithful friend. Brian / October '21.

An anthology in 4 volumes comprising:

Eclectica
Return to Romance
Wanderjahre
Performance 4

ECLECTICA

Copyright © Brian Jackson 2021

The right of Brian Jackson to be identified as author of this work comprising the four collections of poems in this anthology, and including the 'Aftermath' works in progress has been asserted by him in accordance with the Copyright, Designs and Patents Act 1988

All Rights Reserved

No reproduction, copy, or transmission of this publication may be made without written permission.
No paragraph, line or verse of this publication may be reproduced, copied or transmitted save with the written permission or in accordance with the provisions of the Copyright Act 1956 (as amended).

Any person who does any unauthorised act in relation to this publication may be liable to criminal prosecution and civil claims for damage.

ISBN 9798706644345

CONTENTS

FOREWORD 11

ECLECTICA

1 - Of life and Love	13
Judy on a summer night	14
To Judy, a promise	14
Waiting for Judy	16
An age of pity	18
He left	20
The mourners	21
Long waiting's end	21
A farewell	23
Diana	25
To my wife	26
Pretty Molly	27
Urbane	28

2 – Faith	29
The jewel	30
Ahem! Excuse me	31
Stations of emerging Faith	32
Why Cain?	36
Vendetta	37
Galileo	38
I heard God	39
At Ombersley	40
The homecoming	41
After Titanic	45
Going home	46
Windfarm	50
The Vale of Poverty	50

Old World	51
The Castellan	52
The difference	55
3 – Childhood	56
The rain in Spain	57
Treasure re-lived	57
The gift	57
Philip (1)	59
Philip (2)	59
Reflected glory	60
Julia	60
Lucykins	61
Minuet	61
For our children	62
April rain	63
4 – Trains	64
Forgotten dreams	65
In praise of 'Sir Lamiel'	65
The Duchess	66
5 – Africa	72
A Killing Ground	73
All in the April evening	77
The loss of Joss	79
6 - The war to end wars	90
Pals	91
Freunden	93
Ten thousand every day	94
The outsider	97
The Tears of Autumn	98
A reputation	99

7 - A Final Solution	102
The brief illusion	103
The Vanishing	106
Victory march of '45	108
The dentist	111

RETURN TO ROMANCE

En Famille	118
Hands	119
The doubter 'if'	119
To my love	120
Heartsease	121
GWC	122
The thief who comes in the night	123
How can you cry?	125
August 11th 1977	125
How many hours	126
For Jude	127
Upon memory's wings	128
Flutterby	129
God the father	130
Love sans hope	130
What's in a name?	131
My little daughter	132
My son (the great teenager)	132
The colours	133
J'Accuse	133
Ozymandias again	133
The lost souls	134
The Rights of Man	137
Everyman's child	138

This is the way of Modern Man	139
The Irish Fusilier	140
And God created…?	141
The history of Napalm	142

Return to Romance   144

Romance	144
The Knight of No Renown	145
The gardener	153
To Beethoven	153
Fairies	154
Those shopping days	155
Lamenting the muse	156
Trafalgar morning	156
The vase	159
The Old Gods	160
Watcher on the shore	161
Nemesis (1)	162
Nemesis (2)	162
There is silence in the landscape	163
Factory flowered Utopia	163
I want to go back	164
White out	165
The Music of the Spheres	166
An elegy	168

WANDERJAHRE

The Lover   170

The lover	170
My soul's haven	170
In the wake of Siegfried	171
The ghost	171
How can I say?	174

Two lives	175
To my 'Judy-Loo'	175
Home is where the heart is	177
All the world I have	177
On Judy's birthday	178
On sixty-nine	179
To Judy	179
My lifelong love	180
A heaven	181
The garden of my life	181
A declaration	182
A recantation	183
Room 207 – Garda your secrets	184
A distillation of memory	184
Judith by another name	186
On finding the imprint of lipstick	187
I think of you	187
A Valentine for '69	188
The nutcracker, my sweet	189
Wenn trompeten spielen	189

The Cynic   190

Agent Orange, Vietnam	190
Life was bright	191
Let me count the first thousand	192
The great Pretender	193
To the town-hall princes	194
The Mountebanks	195
Mine eyes have seen too much	196
I know what I know – I think	197
How many bled?	198
The fate of man	199
Reflections on a lost career	200
Home thoughts across The Great Divide	200

The Idealist 201
A good day's life 201
The herd – a terminal experience 202
Riding the wind 203
Minstrel Boy 204
A Midsummer nights 205
An die music 206
Back to the Amazon 207
Foolish haste 208
Life's sad regrets 209
Beyond the veil 210
The 'Few' 211
The 'Sheaf' 211
Take me to the mountains 212
The patriot's gift 212
Entropy 214
The shallow, fatuous fool 216
Mystic mist 217
The age of Enlightenment 219
The spaceman 220
18 point 7 billion 222
The protective veil 224
The life we aspire to 224

PERFORMANCE 4

English above all 227
Requiem 228
Let's face reality 230
Eden re-visited, Eden reviled 231
Oh my dear child 232
Earth Mother 234
Elegy in a country car-park 235
The Shepherd's Wheel 236

In the trenches	239
We two	240
Love's joys recalled	241
Love's dream	242
What a difference a day makes	242
I believe	244
Sweet memory's song	245
To friends	246
Memory's heritage	247
I will, I do	249
On 'Judy-Loo' at seventy-two	249
Billy	250
Birthsong	251
September dreams	253
The spirit lives on	254
The mission	255
A moment's hesitation	256
Memorial	259
Love's dialogue	259
The deep	260
Love divined?	260
Speed me on my journey	261
On Rainbow Hill	261
For Audrey	262
I love you	263
Life's remembered love	264
The game	265
Oh may they never stop	265
The more I think	266
The old house groans	266
I haven't ceased	267
Big Bang	267
St Swithins 1991	268
The birds, the bees	269
The Angel	270
Dog eat dog	270

The dark 271
Love's riddle 272
Who will speak? 273
Reflections on a lifetime's love 274
The dance of love 274
When you go to sleep 275
Love's joys recalled 275
I am looking for a headstone ....;. 276
A sense of nostalgia 277
Oh Judy ....…................. 278
The Meeting 278
Taught by Love 279

Appendix 280
Aftermath 284

* * * * * * * * * * *

Foreword

This anthology is a comprehensive collection of all my poems, from my earliest as a teenager through the ones written at different stages throughout my life. Over the years they have been collated into four volumes in rough chronological order from the earliest to the latest. But it should be noted that there is no rigid break between the close of one volume and the next. Indeed, some poems from an earlier period have found their way into a later one. But that doesn't really matter, for it may be that the reason lies in their fitting the general theme. But wherever possible I have dated the poems, and this also gives a general chronology.

Within the volumes you will find poems grouped under generic headings reflecting the particular subject (or anxiety!) I was pre-occupied with at the time of writing: thus 'En famille', 'The Final Solution' etc…

A large part of my poetry stands as a tribute to Judy, my wife. It may be unfashionable in this current age of gender equality, independence and gender confusion but I have basked in the love of my wife since the day I met her and my love for Judy remains a vibrant, everlasting emotion, expressed in myriad ways throughout this collection.

Finally I began to realise whilst editing this lifetime's endeavour that the poems also reflect the changes that evolve in one's own outlook as time passes. Thus whilst in no way autobiographical, 'Eclectica' does represent a view of the poet's changing world and the society he inhabits. Above all – for good or bad – a poet should be truthful in the thoughts and ideas he expresses, for poetry exerts a powerful wider influence.

Brian Jackson
2021.

ECLECTICA

The early poems.

1 OF LIFE AND LOVE

Without love there is no life; no life worth living. True love illuminates and inspires. And whilst it is gentle and compassionate it also has the capacity to raise jealousy and passions. But it always transcends mere logic and simple reason and causes the pathway of our lives to take unexpected and unlooked for turns.

Life is a journey. Sometimes the path is straight and clear; at other times the journey is difficult and beset by storms. But just as summer days must give way to autumn, so the storms must sooner or later blow themselves out and calm weather return. The secret lies in having the emotional resilience to avoid foundering and sinking on the rocks of life.

Friendship and love. These are the greatest of all shelters, providing warmth, support and comfort. They give confidence to see a future beyond the mundane. Without these, life is a barren wilderness.

JUDY ON A SUMMER NIGHT
(1969)

Isn't it time that I told you again,
I love you?
Now that the evenings are warm and
Light and the scent of the flowers fills
The night, while the moths flutter up to
The window light.

And we sit at our ease
In the warm summer breeze
And the hay-fever's tickling
And making me sneeze.
Sitting and talking,
Just knowing you're there,
Smelling the perfume
That drifts through your hair;
The long years of friendship
We're lucky to share…

So isn't it time that I told you again,
Quite simply,
'I love you.'

TO JUDY, A PROMISE
(1978)

Not far away,
 Not far away
Are others we had loved.
 They are in the gold and brightness
Of a summer field
 Set against the dark

Of deep surrounding
  Wood,
The tumbling cloud
  In blue expanse
       Above.

Their Smile
  Is in the warmth
Of high midsummer day;
  Their kiss
The sun
  Full upon
       My face.

And, in the cool and silent
  Intimacy of night
Where Eternity approaches
  So close;
In breathless silence
  Feel their touch.

Unseen beyond
  The veil of earthly thing
Where we cannot see out,
  They peer within.
So please recall, when I am gone
  And you remain,
In birdsong, woods and languid
  Summer airs, is how
    We'll meet
       Again.

WAITING FOR JUDY
(1972)

'He was always there, poor old
   Soul,' she said pointing at the
Empty bench against the shrubbery. Then
   Pursing her lips and drawing
Herself together, she folded her arms
   Across her chest. 'Sometimes he'd
Sit there for hours, just sitting there
   All by himself.' Sniff.
'And the children,' said her friend
   With prim charity. 'He was always
Watching the children. Well – I mean,
   You hear such things don't you!'
'Sometimes I think the only thing he
   Ever cared for was the birds,' rejoined
The first. 'He was always feeding 'em
   You know.'
And she was drawn tight again
   With half an eye
On her children at play.
   'No, I didn't know that. What
All alone?'
   'Oh yes,' she said, 'Lived all alone
He did. Nobody to talk to but
   The birds.'
'Well,' and leaning close, in confidence,
   'What can you expect?' closer now,
The lascivious secret out, 'They say he was
   Going a bit funny you know.
I sometime used to see him
   Down here, watching the sky,
Mutterin' to himself.
   Well it's not natural is it…?'
'Still,' said her friend as the children

Came along, 'it's probably for
The best. Don't like to speak ill of
　The dead. Poor old soul.'
And they went their separate ways.

Poor old soul. Sitting there day after day.
　Watching with bittersweet happiness
The children at their play.
　And the cocky little sparrows,
Shy at first
　Who after a while
Waited for your coming,
　Then burst
Into loud and fluttering
　Chatter as they fought for your bounty.
And the memories that lingered with you
　As you waited, to hear her voice
And see the image of her face
　Hidden in the changing pattern of the sky.

So many days since you felt
　The cool softness of her hand,
Grown weak and gnarled with age.
　Oh Judy, Judy you are always with me
In the air and in the sound
　Of children's laughter…
And he waited through the long,
　Long summer days for her approach
Whilst the oblivious people
　Slyly watched,
Pointing behind his back.

Until the day she came for him.
　And he left the suspicious people
Whom he had long since abandoned;
　And with the sound of happiness

Ringing in his ears, he took her hand,
   And passed into the brighter
     World of love....

AN AGE OF PITY
A conversation piece
(1972)

'WE'LL HELP THE OLD `MAN
  AS MUCH AS WE CAN,
(YOU KNOW HE'S DONE WELL,
  HE'S EXCEEDED HIS SPAN
OF THREE-SCORE AND TEN);
  HE'S A VERY OLD MAN.
SO WE HAVE TO ALLOW
  (THOUGH GOD
KNOWS IT'S A STRAIN)
  FOR THE FACT THAT HE'S JUST
WET HIS BED ONCE AGAIN.'

The world has become a huge and silent
  Emptiness.
Like the slow and heavy motion of
  A dream.
And, as I lay here and watch, the tiny
  Businesses of my life are observed
With the tediousness of a headache.
  Familiar faces of familiar people
Appear and bustle, then depart
  To their greater world.

'WELL HE CAN'T GO MUCH LONGER,
HE CAN'T LAST FOREVER;

(REALLY IT WOULD BE A BLESSING)
    HOWEVER – WE'LL JUST HAVE TO COPE
BUT YOU KNOW, IT'S NO JOKE.
    "I'M JUST GOING TO PUT IN THESE
BEDSHEETS TO SOAK!"'

'Thank you.' I said, oh – so long ago,
    For the comforts and essentials you
Provided.
    But words and deeds endlessly repeated
Become, in time, debased.
    So although I rely upon your various ministries
I have to cease
    Before my conversation becomes
A long and craven, 'Thank you.'

So don't resent my lack
    Of expressed thanks.
They were said with originality and meaning
    So many years ago.
And don't resent the inconvenience
    Of my infirmities.
I can still see more than eyes can tell.
    And there is no comfort in diluted love.

HE HASN'T A CLUE
    AND HE CAN'T GET ABOUT,
AND YOU REALLY CAN'T CHAT
    WHEN YOU'RE HAVING TO SHOUT
- 'I SHAN'T BE A MINUTE' –
    WELL WHAT CAN YOU DO?
HE'S OLD AND HE'S DEAF
    AND HE'S TURNED EIGHTY-TWO.

I feel a young man still,
    Trapped within the confines

Of my age.
   And although I will myself
A steady hand, it trembles
   With the effort. (Why do you
Whisper and point it out?)
   Do you know I still have hopes to
Be fulfilled? I did once but now
    I can't remember...
It's cold out today.
   Well it looks like it...
It's been raining.

I'm alright, I'm alright.
   Where are you going?
Well don't forget my pills.
   No, I'm alright, I shall be alright now...
Where's my stick...?
   .... I'll have a doze....

HE LEFT
(For Terry, who left us)

He left his home,
   He left his car;
He left his wife of countless years.
   He left a breath
Then breathed no more,
   And left us to our mortal fears.
He left us memories to share;
   He left a presence in the air.

THE MOURNERS

'It can't be just forty quid
　That made him do what he did!'
So they surmised in whispers
　And whispered in groups;
Embroidered experiences,
　Things they had seen
Until it made sense
　(What they said, 'must have been!)
And satisfied now that they'd all shed some light
　On the faults he'd committed
Which led to his plight;
　Serene in the knowledge they'd put
His life right
　They left,
　　　His memory in respectful tatters!

LONG WAITINGS END
1977

Like old and waxed and polished wood
　Memories of love and pleasure were
Soaked deep within his mind.
　So that, sitting in their oft-shared room,
Where streaming sunlight fell
　Upon drifting motes of dust
Bright against the cool shade, he recalled
　The sound of conversation and moods
They shared so long ago…
　So long ago…

And long winter evenings, dark and
   Curtained against the fitful wind without,
And the shadows away into deep corners
   Beyond the lamps' glow, he conjured again
The coolness of her hand, the soft,
   Scented warmth of her presence
As the music they had loved filled
   The gently living room.

'Why,' he said, sensing a sudden close
   Companionship,
'She is here.'
   And he raised his reluctant eye to
The dark corners beyond the field of light.
   But the room was as before. Silent as before
Filled only with the sweet flow of music
   And heavy with his thoughts of lost love.

But though he tried to ignore it
   She would not be denied.
She is there.
   She is there! Tangible almost as the dust
That lies along the skirting boards,
   A foothold down upon the darkness.

'Do you believe in ghosts?'
   'Why no.' And they laughed a little
At his fancy.
   'Nor do I,' he replied and took it no further.
But he did enjoy those special nights, waiting
   In the world of winter evening.
For he knew she was there.

She knew when his wait was over, for had she not
   Watched unseen from the shadows
And shared his comfort?

   And he saw her, real and ethereal, and
Watched with fascination, the music
   Filling his ears and mind.
'Come,' she said and without a sound
   He entered into her world whilst around him
The room
   And lamp
      And furniture
Became unreal and fading as he took her hand,
   The cool firm hand of fond memory
And departed, leaving only the music,
   The dust upon the skirting board
      And his lifeless form,
Sublime and content upon the chair...

A FAREWELL
Paris 1792 – The Terror
(1971)

There are so many things that I wish I'd not said
   And so many days gone to waste.
There are so many days when I'd send you away
   With a sad look of hurt on your face;
When you tugged at my hand,
   When you wanted to play
And I didn't have time
   At that hour on that day.

Now it's all gone
   And there'll be no reprieve,
(this isn't the way that I wanted to leave).
   There isn't the fear as expected, or grief
Just a heart-beating tension

That gives no relief.
It stays with you day after day after day
    And it numbs your last hours
As the days roll away.
    But I just want to talk to you,
        And gaze on your face
            And see the light in your eyes....

While I try to recapture
    The days that I lost
So carelessly, thoughtlessly,
    Much to my cost,
Will you ever know
    (Though you'll see me no more)
How I wept for those days
    Huddled there on the floor?

Do you see the same sunlight as I?
    Do you see how it bursts from the sky?
How the clouds catch the goldenlight
    Silver and blue...
There are so many things
    That I'd wanted to do.
But we're rattling and jostling
    And lurching along
Through the uncaring rabble
    That hurry and throng
Just to see us go past
    To be there at the last.

Oh! just let me hear one last birdsong,
    Just let me smell a sweet briar.
Oh, just let me see my dear children again
    In the warm cosy glow of a fire...
But it's passing too fast
    And this pitiless day

Must grow old without me
   For here I must stay.

And there's soot on the chimneys
   And buds on the trees
And woodsmoke and insults
   Are borne on the breeze.
And there's straw on the planking
   And blood on the floor
And panic and breathlessness
   (Only one more!)
And they're binding my arms
   And the time's whirling on,
And the scaffold
   And tumbrils
     And morning
       Are –

DIANA
(September 6th 1997)

 A pall of silence
   And stillness in the land.
 Life suspended,
  Bustle ended,
 Waiting,
  Contemplating.

 Slow movement in the passing crowd,
  A murmur.
 A name! –
  Where before
 It had been joyful,

   Loud –
Only weeping,
  Only crying
At the image, at her dying.

Oh woe for us, a nation in distress
  Who mourn the passing of
Our beautiful Princess.

TO MY WIFE
(MY DEAREST LIFELONG FRIEND)
(1968)

Give me happiness and love;
  That's all I ask.
But most of all give me your love
  For then happiness will follow.

In love with you I'll be your friend
  And love you 'till the very end.
I'll share your doubts as you will mine,
  Our lives will join and intertwine.
And one in both and both in one
We each will be support and help,
  Each for the other one.

With you my wife,
  My dearest friend,
Give me your love
  And I will love you
'till the very end.

And when it comes

   -that sad and bitter end –
When I have lost my dearest, lifelong friend
   What is there left?
It's not enough to cry.
   I'll go into a dark and shrouded room,
And think of all my happiness with you,
   And close my eyes
      And die.

PRETTY MOLLY

I first saw Molly
   'neath her brolly
Waiting for
   The homeward trolley.
Next I saw her
   In the sun
But – with her mum;
   She couldn't come.
Now she's with me
   On the beach,
Bikini clad
   And within reach.

URBANE
(1965)

Give me food and give me drink
   And take me from this kitchen sink
With greasy pots and dirty pans,
   And scratchy, rough dishwater hands.
Oh for a mansion in a park.
   To wake up listening to a lark,
With serving maidens, crisp and white
   To serve up every day's delight.
I'd like a coach and horses too
   (A Rolls-Royce Silver Ghost would do).
Racing stables, winning teams,
They're the things that make my dreams.

Instead I look around and see
   The dreary grim reality.
A city's ancient worn-out slums
   With snotty kids and worn-out mums.
Peeling paint and missing slates,
   Dock and chickweed, broken gates.
Curling pins and plastic shoes,
   Husbands smelling of the booze;
Mild and bitter, ale and stout,
   Quarrelling and falling out.
Lotto! Pools that never win;
   Tea and dinner from a tin.
What a bloody state we're in!

2 FAITH

By its very nature faith is indefinable. It is essentially spiritual and transcends the physical world. It defies logic and reason.

Is the above true? Of course, for there is no other way to account for the triumph of the individual over adversity. And faith is extraordinarily powerful. It conceives outcomes not as 'if' but 'when'. It can turn implacable opposition into co-operation. And it is not constrained by human considerations of finite time.

Faith provides the resilience to endure the unendurable; the conviction to achieve the unachievable and the patience to tolerate the opposing convictions of others. It enables us to look at our ideals, surrounded by the imperfections of our world and to have the confidence to continue when the faithless would despair. Faith turns the impossible into achievable reality.

THE JEWEL

I stand like God omnipotent
   And survey with awe and wonder
The sum of my achievement.
   A tiny Universe of worlds
Lies within my reach as
   I wander and peer,
Curious, at each.

And so I tour the unfathomable
   Gulf, a spirit
Within the void,
   And glance and dart,
And gaze
   And start, amazed
At some rare fruitfulness here,
   Or there
The stirring of something
   Strange and rare.
Then on and on
   Like a wandering comet,
Forever condemned to journey
   In the void.

Until I reach my jewel;
   The bright and glowing,
The rich peak of my achievement.
   But as I reach to touch
It with the essence of Divinity
   I fail,
      Pausing
         In bewilderment,
And can only watch
   With dismay

As my little jewel
   Racks itself in torment.
And then pass on
   For a millennium more…

AHEM! EXCUSE ME

What are you doing?

Yes you – I'm talking to
   You.
For have you never gazed
   At the sky
On a clear and crystal night?
   And have you never seen
(Or felt)
   The limitlessness,
The never ending
   Sheer expanse
And loneliness
   Of the lost and wandering
Universe?

This little bubble,
   Earth,
Adrift upon the mightier
   Ocean of the sky
Is all we have
   You and I.
Why,
   We should cherish
And care for it
   (As though our lives depended…)
For they do!

So stand upon the fertile soil
   And gaze again
Upon the cold
   Impassionate darkness,
And think a little
   (As you make a million,
Billion times more poison
   And destruction
Than before),
   What are you doing?

STATIONS OF EMERGING FAITH

REGRET
   The promiscuous rose gave up its scent
      Without a care
   For where it went;
      And out of the skies,
   Before our eyes
      The false rose withers
   And withering,
      Dies.

And how can I tell you the pleasure
   The innocent joy that it gave.
Oh how can we squander such treasure,
   So fragile, so blessed, so brave?

But there will be no blossom tomorrow
   And there will be no scent in the air.
The earth will be barren and sterile,
   The once fertile corner be bare.

MEMORIAM
> Don't mourn the day,
>> Not for the death of me
> Nor even for my brother man
>> Or even thee.
> Only –
>> The innocence of the world
> Swept away.
>> Oh mourn, mourn that looming day.

> Mourn, mourn the day.
>> The death of hope, joy,
> Inspiration, gladness of the heart;
>> The uplifting soul wherein the
> Aspiring happiness of man resides,
>> And falsely led, despairing, dies.

> The rose, as red as rising sun
>> Flared its scented presence,
> The promise, unfulfilled.
>> The singing earth beckoned, joyful,
> Sweet with summers wholesome rain.
>> Never more to yield a distant harvest;
> Lost in the unheard roar of sunrise.
>> Mourn, oh mourn that distant day.

FEAR
> And fearful is the night
>> That once, with nightmares
> Beckoned thee to bed,
>> Now down within the pillow
> And deep in blankets
>> Hide thy head

> From the night!
>> The unforgiving blackness

And looming terror, lurking, creeping,
   Step by stealthy step,
Enveloping, embracing
   In its fearful reaching
It seeps,
   It permeates…

Do not awake!
   Reality is
     Worse than the dreams.

DECEIT

   The worst of all was the arrogance
     Allied with blatant deceit
   That forced nations to feel
     That peace was unreal.
   So we're hemmed
     And condemned
   In a fortress of steel
     While they gorge on their falsehoods
   Until they're replete.

How can I say that I'd lay down my life
   For an obsolete notion of honour?
How can I say that I'd give you away?
   How can I go - when you need me to stay?
Hear me when I say –
   Hear me when I say! –
To march and be killed for another –
   That would be to betray!

The deceit continues, still unheeded.
   Unchecked, the deadly silent dawn
Is seeded.
   'Our foe, the enemy without'
(within?)

    'See how he makes for war.
      So we'll make more.
    Don't be alarmed,
      We will be armed.'

SORROW

    The happy rose
      Unfolds her fragrant head.
    'Hear me, you are to be
      No more, sweet innocent,
    But blighted, to carry only sorrow
      Where once the bee alighted.'
    And the heavens wept their final tears
      Before the flaring sunrise of infinity.

REVELATION

    I see your fear, your trembling hand,
      The closed look of your eye.
    Optimism, gone with happiness
      Upon the broken promises of
    mankind.
    Then touch my hand, for
      I am your haven and your friend.
    I am your fortress, bound with Love.
      I am your rock, your harbour wall,
    Your shelter from the storms which rage
      About the world.

    Only believe.
      Querulous?
    Why? – for the road ahead is perilous?

    Listen to the ceaseless stirring of the
    wind;
      The pattern of a ripple on the sea,
    The endless infinity of night,

The world, the beauty, the miracle of
Inspiration.
Above all, the thread of love
Binding me to thee.
And believe.

Believe in Love,
  Believe in Grace,
Believe in Hope,
  Believe in Faith.
Believe in Me.

WHY CAIN?

When you and I
  And all the rest
Can love with so much ardour;
  And when we all are able
To show such care
  And kindness;
And the joy of giving
  Brings
Such fulfilment to both,
  (He who gives
As well as he who receives)
  Why – when we are capable
Of such nobility
  Faith
  And honour –
Why does my brother
  Hate me so?

VENDETTA

If I were to say I was going to kill
   Not just for pleasure
But measure for measure
   'How would you know' –
(I hear what you ask)
   'That the actions I'll take
Is the same as the sin
   Carried out against me,
For me to kill him?'

Why is death so essential
   To redeem every ill
That is haunting me still?
   For a lifetime of slights
And advantages gained
   At my naïve expense
And with no recompense
   For a life that's destroyed
As I'm cast in the void.

Well – someone must pay!
   I must find a way
To hit back at random,
   If it means to abandon
All innocent notions I had
   Of fair play.
So I'm lost
   And I grope
For a glimmer of hope
   Every day.

But like sea on a beach
   It's just ebbing away

Whilst the world all around
   Is heedless of me
And my plight.
   So I lay awake restless
And plot
   Through the night.
And nobody knows the danger
   As the hate seethes within.
For I must purge and release
   All the anger which kills…

When and where?
   And who?
You'd be surprised.
   And he will too!

GALILEO
(Galileo forced to recant the truth of what his telescope revealed)

I am Galileo Galilei
And I see what I see.
I am Galileo
Do you see?
For the thoughts within my head
Were put into words instead
But they were better never said.
Oh woe for me.

My hateful name is Galilei;
It is full of hate for me,
I am dumb…
And cannot see!
From the thoughts within my mind

I must make myself be blind.
Oh verité though art unkind.
Ah, pity me.

You mayn't speak to Galilei
Nor may he speak to you.
Discredited! Alone,
Condemned to be.
For on looking through my glass
I thought I saw the Old World pass
For there was a greater Mass
For all to see.

I am Galileo Galilei
And I see what I see;
I am Galileo!
Oh let me see.
But they hide the truth away!
I must recant all I say!
Meanwhile ignorance holds sway,
Condemning me…

I HEARD GOD

Cool,
  Cool upon a hilltop
Beneath the starry night I saw –
  What shall I say?
Why, nothing
  But stars twinkling
Bright and seeming close.

Endless,

    Endless the sky
Reared over me.
    A small cleansing breeze,
The barely rustling trees.
    No horizon, darkness
All around.

I heard?
    God
Speak within my heart.
    I heard?
The joyful sounds
    Of His kingdom, clear
In the silence all around.

And dared?
    To look no further,
For He was there.

Close to God,
    Upon the hill
I remained,
    Content and still,
Safe within the night.

AT OMBERSLEY

I walked amongst the unkempt mounds
    Beneath a broken sky.
I paused; just lichen covered gate,
    The monuments and I.
Standing beneath the swaying yew
    I dwelt upon my life with you.

The echoes of the distant past;
  The sweep of history's great events
Came to me as I lingered there,
  In silence by the litchen fence.
The sweep of horsemen, men of state,
  I heard them all beside that gate.

The sullen blooms of yesterday hang
  Brown upon the graves.
For all we know those faceless mounds
  Are vagabonds and knaves.
Yet would I be a yeoman too,
  And share my simple life with you.

THE HOMECOMING

Through all my dreary aches I lay wet
eyed
  And think.
Oh yes, I think of you.
  Pleasant green and pink and blue, sky
and
Meadows, lilting music.
  But most of all there's happiness –
        And you.

Not here within this black abyss, this hell
  Removed, far far away
From care and thought, stripped of
dignity.
  Am I a man?
        I'm not.

   The merest brute of flesh
And bone who lies beneath the earth –
  Shut off, enclosed,
          Away beyond the reach of sky.
I live in darkness, I am told, because of
  The offence I give the eye.

I am not! – Look at me! Look at me!
  Look at me! Oh God where are you?
I will believe.
  How can You regard me in this state of
Anarchy in nature and turn away
indifferent?
  I am a man! (I tell myself).
        I am! I am!

The fit has passed.
  I was nearly free to roam in spirit
Back toward my home.
  And then my nose betrayed me and by
The smell of rotten stinking rags and
straw
  And mildew spreading out upon
The floor
  I came back to my prison cell
       Once more.
Passion spent and growing faint,
  And fainter yet with each successive fit
      I did
         Return
           To lie and weep
            Myself
               To troubled sleep.

What did I used to be?

What madness led me here? Away from
Happiness and love, where once I had
   Respect and intellect? (Compared to
now!)
What is this world?
   A world within the world I knew
Bounded by the walls of Hades – this
Hell!
   Outside, a world of light and shade
Where flowers smell,
   And oceans beat their surf upon the
shore,
And sun sets gleaming in a gaudy sky
   And the wind can blow your thoughts
Freely away,
   Away across the ocean
           White with spray,
                   Skimming across the sea.

Its happening again!
   Dragged up – awake? Asleep?
The stairs are steep,
   My legs and feet
           Bruised.
No time to catch the step we race aloft
again.
   Its odd, I know what's there but
somehow
It doesn't seem to matter – only...
   I can't go on;
           Not another time.
           Don't do it to me again...
It's been so many times and I don't know
           What they want.

Abused

And used.
        Mocked and beaten,
                Bruised and bloodied…
Once again you have my body but you cannot
  Get inside – can you?
He must have seen the look of triumph that
  Barely – for an instant
Managed to gleam through my shuttered eyes.
  But no matter
        For you cannot touch my soul.

No – but they have the rest, and this
  Is the last time! And they will do with me
What they will.
  I can see them.
        Ranged about this poor broken body
Like wild beasts at the kill.
  And they maim and beat,
        Desperate to reach…
And pain comes in huge, gasping bolts.
  Again and then again,
        Surging and receding
                Like the ocean tide.
But I am free!
  I lay and watch them with their hideous enthusiasm…

Can you hear me?
  From where I lay, from where I'll never leave
  A simple thread of hope my mind can

weave
And cast aloft; searching out across the world
  To reach
         For you.
Listen – stand still and listen –
  To me…
What - do you not believe?
  You know it's me.
It is, it is,
  It's me.

And I see you pause in your step and think,
  Searching for a half-remembered….
Something.
  You are remembering aren't you.
And while the wind blows
  Uncaring through your hair
You feel a certain light
  And happiness in your memory,
For I am with you
  There.

AFTER TITANIC

He'd tried to swim a little;
    He'd even tried to shout
But like a piece of storm-tossed wrack
    The waves flung him about.

He drifted as the iciness
    Sent cramp into his limbs
And sank, before he started up

        And tried once more to swim.
    But weariness o'er came him
        And his mind turned to within.

He heard the sound of music
        As the waves closed on his head.
He heard the sound of symphonies,
        The sounds he thought were dead.
A long forgotten,
        Loved and treasured,
              Full concerted sound.
Oblivious of the iciness
        In pleasure he was drowned.

GOING HOME
(1966)

1.

It seemed just like the summer days
  Of endless heat and burning rays,
A magic, childhood time.
  And travelling, cosy in the car
His journey's end ahead so far,
  Gently climbing to the hills
Into the rays of evening sun
  (His journey scarcely half begun)
His aching mind he fills.

With wonder and delight,
  As in the fading light
The hoar-frost on the spiky hedge
  Catches the light and gleams and glistens,
And as the jaded traveller listens
  No sound is in the air.

Just the white and powdered grass
   That stiffly stands as though its glass
(And if on foot you were to pass
   You'd feel the icy trinkets smash
Beneath your frozen feet).
   So ever more reluctant, upon the magic road
The traveller turns a wistful eye
   At the freezing scenery passing by,
And high and higher and still more high
   The traveller climbed and gradually slowed
Up on the snaky hillside road.

Despite the cloudless, sunny winter day
   The pine plantation, white and ghostly, lay
Laden with an unrelenting rime
   Of crystal frost.
And to the travellers mind, all sense of time
   Was lost.

Near the summit of the road,
   Between two shoulders of the hill
He stopped the car – and listened.
   And around him all was still.
Too cold to stir the wind
   Out from his lair;
Just the icy stillness
   Hanging there.
And the traveller sat rigid in his car,
   Thinking…

2.
The shadows of the night started
   To creep down the dark ravine
As the traveller stepped out from
   His car (and locked it safely),
Whilst the light was still sufficient

For the sheep-path to be seen.

He began to climb away into the hills,
  Puffing now and panting
As he hurried up from where he'd left his car.
  His hands were wet and glowing
From the frosted grass; his breath
  In great puffing clouds vanished in the air,
And the cold began to filter through his
  Clothing to his skin.

At last he reached the top, surveying
  The monstrous rolling backs
Of the high surrounding hills.
  So he huddled into a clammy hollow,
Drawing his coat around him,
  And settled down to wait...
And it wasn't long in coming.
  It froze his feet uncomfortable in his shoes
And froze his knee-joints stiff and solid
  So that,
When at last
  He wanted to stretch and move
His legs, the will had gone.
  And the night fell on him
Like a freezing black blanket...

The cold became a pain and
  A kind of panic seized him and
He stumbled, awkward and disjointed
  From his hole.
Until he fell, down among the grassy heather mounds.
  And rolling over he gazed up at
The unrelenting stars,
  Becoming less conscious of the cold,
And wondered where the others were,

    And what they would be doing
And had they had the time to miss him yet?

Unstirring as he lay there, a subtle
  Rime of frost began to coat his clothes
And pinch his ears.
  While the unrelenting numbness penetrated
To his core and the traveller began to lose
  His fears,
So that while his body froze
  Mem'ries in his mind arose
And he went back to his childhood
  Down the years.
To his happy sunny childhood
  And the hop-fields in the haze;
All the friends he used to play with
  In those happy carefree days.
Of how he held his daddy's hand
  So proudly by his side,
And throwing stones and fishing,
  And going for a ride;
The magic and excitement leading up to
  Christmas week – and a little
Tear of sadness welled and froze upon his cheek.
  Laying there, remembering,
And hearing distant cars,
  He went away to happiness again up in the stars.

3.

He was brought down from the hillside
  Frozen into the rigid form of death,
And bundled in a brittle heap, blanketed in the van.
His wife was overcome
  With bewilderment (and tributes)
But while the others soon forgot
  She lay awake at nights, and wondered

In her haggard mind
  'What made him want to die?'
And then in her bewilderment
  She too would softly cry…

WINDFARM

High,
  In desolation and sinister aloofness.
Implacable,
  Silently reaching and clawing
At the clouds.
  Gleaming in sunlight,
Shadowless and bright
  Against the sky,
The blades
  Rotate, rotate,
Cutting in frustration
  At the air
Whilst the wind
  Howls past in mockery.

THE VALE OF POVERTY

Hate the darkening world!
  The rushing clouds, tumbling darkly,
Compress and battle with the wind,
  Who shrieks
  And speaks in moans,
Bewailing his lofty solitude,
  Swirling in a rush upon the stones

And flinging spiteful grit
  Beneath the black-massed heavens
Upon the moor.

The millstone stands within
  Its broken frame.
The flinty road winds on its
  Desolate way.
Dark night begins his onslaught
  Once again;
Retreating into shadow goes the day.

Advancing wind-borne shadow,
  Swift climbing on the hill
Relentless, pursues the remnants of
  The day that linger still.
'Black', cries the night;
  Shrieking with glee
The wind sweeps high upon the moor
  To catch its prey,
The haggard poor, with poverty
  Round them pinned.

OLD WORLD

Look at the world. This sad old world
  Cries tears of rain.
And in the clouds
  The thunder growls
And rumbles on and on in savage pain.

Hark to the wind; unyielding wind

   That howls along
And pushes with relentless force
   And no sign of remorse
'till all is gone.

Ponder the sea, the secret sea
   That never sleeps.
From lashing storms new dreams are born
   To carry surging currents ever on
Through silent deeps.

Gaze at the sky; the empty sky,
   Indifferent to you or I.
Whose limitlessness fills the eye
   With hundred thousand million stars
Which in our fancy fondly gaze
   And wonder at our quaint old ways
Of sundering
   Our only living place;
      This Earth of ours,
         This world,
            This sad old world.

THE CASTELLAN

So fair and full of promise it had seemed
   Across the serene lake where placid
swans
Glided in the reeds and swallows
   Dipped and flew.
Its towers, o'er looked by noble banners
   Drifting languidly in the breeze,

Were built (as was the rest) of golden
   Honey-coloured stone.
Before the door, a noble portal leading
   From a quarried quay there rode
A barge of red and gold.
   This then, this fabled happy place
I gazed upon, was to be for some short
   Time my charge, my new abode.

We barely had the time to stand and gaze,
   Treading the grassy water's edge to
Where the jetty thrust into the lake when,
   From the island quay we saw the barge
Begin to glide.
   What beautiful, majestic sight!
The craft, its paint and giltwork gleaming
   In the golden evening, with oars
That dipped and lifted in determined
   Rhythm, shedding spangled drops
As it cruised upon the glossy water.
   Behind, the mighty island fortress stood
Lone and splendid, stark against
   The glowing sky.

We stepped aboard and stood
   High in the lofty poop, swelling with
Proud anticipation as we steadfastly
   Approached in silence.
Out, toward those lofty towers and
   Banners fair, surveyed and studied
By the ever growing throng who lined out
   On the walls. And then we were ashore.

Stepping from the craft as the mighty
   Studded door withdrew inwards and
The portal grille ascended out of sight.

   The brazen sound of trumpets, in fanfare
Resounded out across the new-rippled
lake
   Reverberating in the distant forest
Round about. Our entry to the Court,
   Receiving warmth and loyalty at
Every step, a triumph, was complete.

Oh how sad! How sad to recollect
   That brilliant, happy hour. How long
ago?
A week, a year, or more? All gone!
   Still lies the lake, its crumbling jetty
Fallen into disrepute.
   No longer are there swans to glide
Between the shore and that cracked
   And broken ruin.
Not even sunset lingers there to soften
   And romanticise the wretched pile,
But hard driving rain and lowering clouds,
   Scudding fugitives as I am now.
Disgraced and hunted, driven from this
   Dismal place with ears and mind oblivious
To the sad and doleful mournings of
   The past, I turn and pick my phantom
Way in sadness from the sight.

THE DIFFERENCE

The hardest part of dying was the living
At the end,
And the fighting and clinging onto life.
And facing the reality
Of desperate humanity.

For all the other nonsense
Doesn't matter any more,
Like the sensibilities that mark
The wealthy from the poor
As I sprawl in disarray and gasp
My life out on the floor.
And the curious and sorrowful
Crowd helpless at the door,
Casting about for something
Which they know they cannot give.

And it isn't light that's fading
(no matter what they say)
But there's something going from me,
Something different today,
That I've never felt before
As I lay here on the floor.
And they're trying – oh they try
When they see the slightest flicker,
With renewed hope and vigour
(on their part, not on mine).
Now a final subtle flourish
And I quietly slip away,
    Leaving you gazing
At what used to be
And trying to see
              The difference…

3 CHILDHOOD

Can we ever recapture it? Can we ever relive it? We may try through our own children, perhaps more successfully with our grandchildren. But childhood is a land to which we can never return. For unlike the snake which sheds its skin, we cannot shed the accumulation of knowledge and experience gained as we progress through adult life.

In our wistful nostalgia for the lost age of innocence all we can do is remember. But the images are no longer true; memory is a distorting glass and we yearn for what we thought it was. Do we remember our passions and juvenile cruelties? Or is it that we yearn to shed the hideous burdens of the adult world to revisit the land we thought we lived in?

Childhood nostalgia is a deception we indulge in like an opium smokers dream. What we see when we look at our children cannot be the reality of their world for they exist in a separate universe, a one-way access system in which they journey progressively into our world with no way back. All we can do is help them to make the transition successfully and hope meanwhile, that what we observe is close to the reality for them.

THE RAIN IN SPAIN

The rain in Spain
  Runs down the drain
Where once it filtered off the plain.
  In France it drives the French insane
(The English too, we're just the same).

TREASURE RELIVED

I want to walk the streets again
  I walked when I was four,
And see her face and hear
  The cries of welcome at her door.

I want to feel the sunlight
  On my young and carefree face.
I want – but it's no use to want,
  For nothing can re-trace.

So let me sit and treasure,
  Re-living in my mind
The life I used to live before,
  The life I left behind.

THE GIFT

Awaken.
  Awaken and softly gaze around
And listen for the blessings
  Of each day.
What's that you say? (from the
  Dull and sleepy mind

That slowly greets the day).
   You look and wait, and listen
But cannot see the blessing?
   Then I say –
Wait and listen,
   Listen hard with me;
There are more senses
   And more sounds
Than a tired mind can see.

Now,
   Recline, relax, that's it, rest on my shoulder
And wait for the sound of blessings
   Which, ever bolder
Creep into the senses of
   This early-morning mind.
Suppressed and joyful
   Bubbling excitement creeps
And then explodes upon us from the room
   Where, offspring of thy womb,
Our children lie.

They gleeful, scampering,
   Bring for us to see those
Expected gifts which Christmas brings
   For them, for you, for me.
But most of all, intangible,
   The gift of love.
Un-tinselled and unwrapped, forever fair,
   In good times and in bad.
This is my fervent prayer:
   Dear God, give me the strength
And will, my family for to care,
   And caring, to remain with them
In love, and hope, and... there.

PHILIP (1)
(1975)

We have – you know – a boy in the house
   (With smoky hair
   And dirty knees)
Who scrambles and fidgets about like a mouse.
   He scuffs his shoes and scatters his toys
(you can tell where he is because of the noise)
   In short, I suppose he's just 'one of the boys.'

But now he's asleep, tucked safe in bed
   (with angel face
   And not a care)
The house is calm and peaceful instead.
   The comics and toys are packed away
(the remains of his supper still on the tray).
   I hope that I helped him enjoy his day.

PHILIP (2)
(1976)

He's only nine –
   A wonderful age, childhood's prime.
Innocent still but very shrewd,
   I told a joke, he said, 'That's rude'.
I wish I had his clarity,
   His innocent hilarity.
I tell myself I must be firm
   And so I guess I'm rather stern,
But still, my son
   We do have fun,
And when your childhood's course is run
   Forgive me please, my gravity.

REFLECTED GLORY

Did you ever know the joy
  Of playing football with a boy
Who's full of fire,
  Who runs and dreams
He's picked for First Division teams.
  He commentates each move he makes,
He dives and scrambles, slithers, skates,
  And though you're older
With more skill
  He'll run you 'till your legs are still.
But on that field you're not his dad,
  Balding, middle-aged and sad;
His bright young eyes
  Re-call your dreams –
He's playing First Division teams.

JULIA
(1976)

What did Julia do today
  While out-and-about on her merry way
With her woolly red coat and her bean-bag frog
  And her golden hair and charming smile?
We went out awhile.

We called in a café for some chips,
  (her eyes lit up and she licked her lips
And filled her orange-juice with salt).
  So she finished up finishing off my tea.
I can't deny blue eyes you see.

We made some stops
    At various shops;
She dropped her bean-bag on the road
    So back we went to fetch the toad,
(we didn't mind our journey slowed)
    She's not yet two.
OK – So what!
    She's the goldenest, prettiest girl I've got.

LUCYKINS

There is a girl called 'Lucykins'
    As sweet, as sweet can be.
And Lucykins, this Lucykins,
    She sits upon my knee
And puts her soft and pink-nailed hand
    So gently into mine.
Oh Lucykins, sweet Lucykins
    I'll be your Valentine.

MINUET

There, in a dense and misty wood
    Where the overhanging trees
Rise brooding high above
    The fresh, green dappled glade
Is where we stood.

Silently, silently came the drift
    And heartfelt rustle of a
Faerie wing, borne on the air…

All in the haze of a hushed
And breathless dream.

She is there,
　She is there, unseen upon the
Sparkling dewfresh grass; Lucy,
　Bright-eyed and blind with innocence.
Dancing, dancing, step and point
　With graceful turn and sweep;
Turn and point and pirouette
　In the faerie spell of sleep.
All to the silent music of the forest
Like a clockwork marionette
　Upon the flowers.

And, as the brightness fades
　Do not weep
For the lingering memory of Lucy remains
　In the sweet
Dancing innocence of childhood.
　Elusive, like the scent
Of summer flowers.

FOR OUR CHILDREN

There were swans upon the river,
　　　Ducks were dipping in the water
As I walked upon the meadow
　　　With my daughter's little daughter.
And the water sparkled brightly
　　　And reflected in the sun.

And the air was still and scented
　　　As we turned again for home.

And my spirit soared and lifted
    And my heart was full again
As we walked the dappled shadows
    Back along the scented lane.

And the sun was setting, gleaming
    In the balmy summer's eve
And I fell again to dreaming
    Of the things we might achieve
For my hope is for the future
    And it's there for us to see
In my daughter's little daughter
    Danielle, who's nearly three.

APRIL RAIN

Drip, drip, drip, drip,
    Sparkling droplets
Catching colours
    Dazzle! Dazzling
Tricks of light,
    Tricks of sight.
Look! And look again
    Where fairies splash and play;
Look, look and look again
    They're – was it real? –
They've gone away.
    Just flowers growing
Bright in the border.

4 TRAINS

What a curious fascination the age of steam exerts. I can't explain why. Its mixed up with memories of a world we used to inhabit where modest pleasures held great expectations and a sea-side holiday never disappointed.

The arrival of the great locomotive gliding implacably, impressively into the station raised a frisson of excitement. Above the blast of steam as the locomotive simmered at the head of the train, above the calls of porters, the rattle and the chatter of passengers, the sing-song station announcements echoed beneath the station roofs urging us along with unintelligible information. And as the last doors slam there is a bustle of farewells and a rush of final passengers. The whistle pierces the station, the green flag waves, the passengers wave and we are gone beneath a bridge wreathed in smoke…

FORGOTTEN DREAMS

To sleep within the sound of train
   And hear the pulse-beat once again
That echoes in the distant night.
   Within the room, the firebox light,
The fireman's sweat, the muscles strain,
   The surge of midnight parcel train…
And then to sleep, to dream again.

IN PRAISE OF 'SIR LAMIEL'
(11th July 1991)

In gardens and windows,
      On hedgerows and bridges,
By cuttings and layby's,
      In meadows and ridges,
Oblivious to sunburn
      Or harassing midges;
Smiling and beaming
      They're all here again,
Drawn by the impulse to see a steam train.

What do they think
      As they stand in the steam,
With the tang of the smoke
      And the pang of a dream?
For the adults a wave,
      For the children a cheer
As the echoing whistle cries,
      'Lamiel' is here…

They stand in the sunlight
    And watch her surge by
With a lump in the throat
    And an envious sigh.

THE DUCHESS

The cutting – such a solitary place;
  We follow the track between the banks,
Stepping along the oily sleepers,
  Hopping along the rusting track
In the profound silence
  That only deserted industry
Imparts.

There's birds, twittering
  On the fence
And bees are busy
  Among the dense
Weed and flowers
  And tufts of grass
As we pass
  Along the curving track
Beneath the sun.

There's a treasure –
  An old coach bolt,
Square and massive,
  Rusting among the grey-white
Gravel chips of ballast.
  And not a soul.
Used to be though
  - days of yore –

Gangs of navvies,
  Pick and shovel,
Heave and strain,
  Only muscle
To lay the track
  (and step aside)
As distant whistle heralded
  The coming of a train.

But now it's such a private place.
  We stroll at our unhurried pace;
A cinder, and a bolt
  (or two).
Blackbirds set up noisy chatter,
  Butterflies dance erratically
And low across the way
  And the bees are busy
On the bank.

There's a wagon;
  There's a coach.
Beyond them the old worn-out shed.
  Only a branch, a rural line,
Despised perhaps
  In its time
In its prime,
  Not like Crewe South or Polmadie
A Mecca.
  Hardly worth a stop.
A pair of Johnson number 3's
  Oh – and that funny High Peak job,
But still…

Good grief – Look at it!
  Probably an old steam crane
Or a Black 5 if

   They're lucky.
Bit of a backwater all the same.
   Ah there's a bloke with
An oily rag – no doubt
   A volunteer.
I give a shout,
   'Can we go in?'
He points,
   A door set in the dirty wall
In the shade
   Where the oily water,
Stagnant,
   Lays in pools along the track
Rusting rubbish.

He's vanished.
   We carry on, pick our way,
Minding our feet
   And the gloom is sudden, pleasant,
Shady from the heat
   Of the sun outside.
Small and dark, but it
   Smells the same,
Just as memory recalled,
   Steeped in oil and steam
A sort of sweet…
   A railway smell.

Now, mind your coat, there's
   Not much room between
That driving link
   And the grimy wall.
Six driving wheels, a pair at the front;
   They used to use this one
To shunt
   Or else the locals,

A coach or two;
  That would do –
Puffing and trundling
  Back and forth
The fifteen miles or so
  Along the branch.

Ah – here's another!
  We used to see a lot of these…
Shan't be long now, then we'll go.
  Mind that buffer
It's heavy with grease…
  That buffer's OVAL!
Oh look…
  Come and look!
And we stood before her
  Didn't we.
Mute subjects
  In the presence of a 'Duchess'.

Mute and lifeless now
  But looking so, well,
Pleased.
  But her cylinders are
Cold.
  And the polished copper steam pipes
Mere decoration.
  Lined and liveried Crimson Lake
In the dusty shaft of sunlight
  That filters through the roof,
Waiting for life;
  The breath of fire,
The surge of steam,
  The mighty blast of power.
We stand,
  No longer alone.

'Doesn't she look grand.'
  But he replied,
'She'll never run,
  Her insides rotten,
Tubes are gone.'
  So there you are, silent majesty.
But we remember don't we,
  So many years ago…

'Do you want to go to Morecambe?'
  'Well alright, but if I can
I'd like to leave for an hour or so
  And go to this little place I know.'
So they understood and said 'OK'
  And so that is where I was that day,
And after seeing one or two
  Why my proud Duchess,
There was you!

The distant signal rose as well
  When, off to the North
We saw your plume
  And suddenly you
Were engulfed in spume,
  Racing along the water troughs
With just your smokebox door in view
  As you hurtled on us
Wreathed in spray,
  Drenching us all
And then with the
  Pounding steam and smoke…

Kids ran forward, two or three,
  All excitement, just like me.
'Semi!' they cry
  And the track was singing,

The wires were humming
  With the speed of your coming!
And smoke and steam
  And vapoured water
Mingled in your mighty wake
  Until with a whistle and roar
You're through!
  The platform quivers, fittings shake,
Your drenched train hurtles along behind
  Leaving us with shining eyes;
The train recedes,
  The excitement dies.

And the station fell quiet.
  And the swinging lamps came to rest,
And peace descended on the afternoon,
  Just like today…

Oh! – but that first sight
  Of you in full cry.
Six hundred tons from Scotland
  And non-stop all the way.
Why, I would not for all the world
  Have missed you on that day.

5   AFRICA

The sorrows of Africa are compounded by the legacies of white colonial imperialism. Whilst some countries managed to achieve a peaceful transition to independence, many African states descended into tribal warfare and Africa became the playground of mercenary armies. The anarchy of 12th C England was repeated in 20th C Africa.

The obscenity is that whilst mature western democracies pulled out of direct rule, multi-national companies continued to exploit the wealth of Africa with practices that would be deplored on European home territory. Corruption flourished and wars erupted one after the other in this post-colonial continent. And always the arms merchants were there, fanning the flames, following the market.

We become inured to horror and violence when the land is remote, and we are not affected directly. But the personal tragedies are still enacted, sometimes on a scale so vast that individual consequences pass unnoticed. Until an image suddenly hits you and then the memory is fixed forever. But at least we have the consolation of knowing that of course it couldn't happen here…

A KILLING GROUND

With stealth in his movements he
   Pulled aside the leafy branch.
Not too wide, but just enough,
   And indicated by nod of the head
(just a twitch, no more)
   To the other
Who
   Lay with him on the floor;
In a secret, urgent, high
   Tension breath, just a whisper,
Said,
   'There's your killing ground.'
Then back they both slid.

The stealth remained; but with
   Urgency too
They showed the others
   What to do,
And where to deploy their
   Field of fire.
With not a word, just a
   Nod and wink,
Sweep of the arm, you'd almost
   Think
It was a game
   Like we played as children.

Except for the silent bustle
   And the straining of
Each muscle,
   To move the arms
Without a sound;

   To place them stealthily
All around
   With nervous, breathless
Silent haste
   'till they had command
Of the killing place.

And in no time at all it was done.
   And stillness descended
Upon
   The hot and breathless clearing
(save buzzing flies
   Around the hidden men
Peering over the rise;
   Concealed in the bush,
Crouching,
   Lying,
     In the dust).

And the sun grew hot
   As they lay.
Alertness passed to irritation.
   The flies sought them out
As they sweat
   Beneath their shirt
And away across the dirt
   The killing ground
Shimmered in the haze.

Sweated and twitched
   And silently cursed
And, 'Who's got it wrong this time?'
   As the minutes passed
To hours beneath
   The flat pan heat of the sun…

One saw him first!
   Silently moving just beyond a bush,
Beyond the brazen haze
   Where the air buckled, shimmered.
And the man watched his quarry
   Creep slowly from his hiding place
And gaze, with full intent,
   Ahead.
And they looked at each other;
   One without seeing as he stepped out,
Clear, and stood and waited.

All was at peace
   But still he wasn't sure,
Standing head erect,
   Searching in the air
For some hidden sense to tell him
   What he knew.
But the flies buzzed
   And the sun shimmered
Down upon the dry red earth
   And the poor brittle brushwood
(which grew there)
   Cracked and withered.
And in that instant he was lost.
   For he looked at
The things he could see
   And recalled the abstract
Antennae of his instinct.
   And so he stood,
Relaxation evaporating
   The tension of his senses,
Turning to unseen companions behind.

To the unseen watcher
   Lying prone behind his gun

The irritation and the flies
　　Were but a thing of distant memory
As with the stealthiest
　　And tiniest
Shift of an elbow
　　And flinching of shoulders
He lay refreshed and ready.

They came on with a semblance of
　　Alertness
Behind their scout,
　　Heads peering about,
Arms loosely slung
　　With water bottles hung
About their necks, when,
　　Almost to a man
They saw the raised arm,
　　Stiff behind the brittle thorn
DROP! And they KNEW
　　They were in the killing ground,
Falling dead and torn
　　With surprise and din
And racket in
　　Their empty brain…
And as they fell
　　And twitched
　　　　　And bled
They never heard the wider sound,
　　All around
The flurry and slap of wings,
　　The shrill calling of the birds
Which rose as one from
　　All around
The smoking, choking killing ground.

They were stripped

Of arms and badges of
Rank and the odd souvenir
  (or two).
And the echoes died away,
  And the birds returned
To perch and preen.
  And the sun went down
As they remained
  In mutilation
Beneath the cool and starry sky
  In darkness
On the ground
  Alone…

ALL IN THE APRIL EVENING
(1997)

All in the April evening
  In the gentle April air
The light of the gleaming evening
  Cast its shadows on me there.
And the blossoming scents arose again
  From the hawthorne in the scented lane.
And the cries of children at their play
  Came on the air at the close of day.
But the lambs that were weary and crying
  Had a weak and human cry!

Oh why do you show me the things
  I can't help you with?
Why do you show me the horrors of war?
  We look at the images, weep for the victims,
Retreat into comfort and say, 'Never

more.'
  Then we switch off the screen
For its better not seen.

Only –
  All in the April evening
On the road to Kisangani
  In Zaire we saw the residue of
Someone else's army.

For there was a child
  At the side of the road,
Sharing the same April evening as I,
  Too weak to move
Save to half-raise an arm
  And I heard – not a lamb –
But a dying child cry.
  And then – God forgive me –
I passed that child by.
  (just a flick of the switch
Left that child in the ditch).

And the sun set in England
  That same April day
As it set on that child
  As his life ebbed away…

THE LOSS OF JOSS
(Kolwezi, the Congo and the Katanga secession)
(1984)

1

I remember Mrs. Joss
  Dressed in muslin or in cotton,
Wide brimmed hat of straw or lace,
  Just enough to shade her face,
Images I'd thought forgotten.

I remember all her laughter
  At some joke of mine or Joss's
And the help she gave to others,
  To the black kids and their mothers
Never counting her own losses.

I recall the barbecues
  On their sunlit terrace garden,
Houseboys primly dressed in white.
  Joss and I would gently fight
As our drunk opinions hardened.

Expeditions into town,
  Escorts driving through the bush,
Cream teas taken English style,
  Lingering at the club awhile
And then home again – no rush.

I remember with affection
  Harold Joss and Jan, his wife.
But the happy recollection
  Of how they enhanced my life
Bears the mark
  Of something dark.

2

The bungalows were side-by-side
  (they shared a garden wall)
Upon an avenue straight and wide
  With grassy borders trimmed with pride
On which grew palm trees, slender, tall.
  A little bit of Europe
Above all.

For down the dusty avenue
  The lawns and borders bright
Proclaimed the information that
  This area was white!

There was unrest in the hinterland
  And trouble in some town;
It was born of small beginnings
  But the army put it down,
And life returned to normal
  (it couldn't happen here).
Joss said, 'We'll have a barbecue,
  I'll get some steaks and beer.'
So we carried on with what we thought
  Was life just as before
Until that life was shattered.
  Do you want me to say more?

3

Mrs. Joss had sat with me
  Beneath the Oleander tree
With a glass of gin-and-bitters
  And confessed to having jitters.
Looking at the garden party,
  Friends and neighbours, hale and hearty,
Sitting there beneath the tree
  With her hand upon my knee

Jan had voiced her fears to me.

Her hair had borne a golden sheen,
   He eyes were bright, her eyes discreet
And from her head to dainty feet
   She filled my every aching dream.
But - for that, she was Joss's wife
   For her I would lay down my life.

Down beneath the Oleander
   With her hand upon my knee,
Her scent – sweet as a pomander
   From her proximity to me,
Jan gave vent to mounting fears
   That the happiness of years
Must soon go – be swept away.
   'Wait,' I cried, 'you cannot say…'
But her lowly mood persisted;
   As I countered she resisted
'till at last we both gave in,
   Agreed to differ – have more gin.

An oh! - so gentle touch of hands,
   A shared and understanding glance,
Then I returned to gin and Joss
   And she to other guests of course.

4

And now I sit in darkness,
   The darkness of my mind;
More profound, deeper, blacker
   Than a neatly pulled-down blind.
For now I sit in emptiness,
   A deeply hollow void,
In my lonely nights remembering
   The way it was destroyed.

And my days are filled with introspection
   Welling from within,
And my evenings with loneliness,
   The loneliness of gin.
I hear again her voice, the way it used to
   Fill my dreams,
And I hear again the shouting, brutish
   Laughter and her screams.

Each night here,
   Recalling fear
I sit with gin (or maybe beer)
   Trying to dispel
Pictures so carefully
   - so carefully – preserved.
The tragedy, it seems,
   Is fascination with these dreams.

The bedsit door is locked
   And barred against the terrors
Of the English suburbs
   While I wait. (Don't deride
My heavy stick within reach
   By my side),
Alert for wild shadows at the window.
   (Wish I still had the gun, gin's no help!)

Oh my God – they're here! They've come!
   The gun! The gun!
Oh God it's just the trees
   And ivy drooping from the eaves,
Rattling and scraping
   Even here
Where the yellow autumn
   Lamplight glows through innocent

drizzle.
Innocent shadows
  Give rise to fear.

Must get it trimmed back.
  That was a close call;
Need a drink after that.
  Here we go – once more into the night
Dear friends,
  Joss.
And a large one for Mrs. J.
  As you were my dear…
My dear…
  Jan…Mrs. J.
Wish I had my gun
  I'd never see another day.
They don't know what we went through…
  I wish that I could pray…

5

Down the lonely avenue
  Battened down for night,
Down among the lawns
  Among the houses of the white
Where the scented Oleander and hibiscus
  Grew in borders
In the open-plan estate
  (which is open to marauders)
Well, down along the avenue,
  Battened down for night
Came a bunch of drunken rebels
  Who were itching for a fight.

With whisky and gin
  And an arrogant swagger,
With some apprehension,

A sway and a stagger,
With boisterous brutishness
  Pushing and shoving
And swearing and laughing
  And pinching and tugging
They came to the suburb
  Where white man was boss;
They came to the garden
  Of bungalow Joss.

'My God there's someone out there!
  Abdullah fetch the gun.
Well don't just stand there gawping
  At me – go and fetch it. Run!'
I'd gone then to the window
  For a careful look around,
Creeping by the furniture, not to make
  A sound.
Peering through the jalousies,
  Wondering what I'd heard
(perhaps a stray hyena? –
  Don't be so absurd).
But deep inside a growing fear-
  We know the rebel army's here.
There's just the shadows on the lawn.
  Oh where's Abdullah? Where's he
gone?

My God they're coming up the street,
  They're – where's Abdullah? Curse the
man.
They're drunk – How many? Go myself;
  Box of shells up on the shelf;
Now the pistol in the drawer,
  Show those blighters what its for!

In the darkness of the shadows,
   On the moonlit open lawn
Came a stealthy band of soldiers
   (I could just make out their form),
Fanning out in threes and fours,
   Trying windows, skirting doors.
Standing there behind the blind,
   Pistol bravely clenched in fist,
Trying to make up my mind
   How I wished, oh how I wished
That I knew
         What to do.

If I can just keep my nerve,
   Just be ready, in reserve.
Got the gun,
   Should be fun!
Jos'll sort the blighters out;
   Me and Joss - be a rout!
So hiding there in darkness,
   In silence with the gun
I hid in indecision until
   Joss should start the fun…

In swarms
   They cross the open lawn,
Creeping round the dark verandas
   'till a coarse, delighted shout
Revealed the fatal mischance,
   Jan had left the washing out!

The sight through whisky-laden eyes
   Of lace and silk (small woman's size)
Contoured for waist and breast and thighs
   Gave rise to visions, which gave rise
To thoughts of quite a different prize.

In sport they took the garments down
   And breathless, laughing passed then round -
And yelling all the time for more
   As some were worn, and others tore –
Advanced as one on Joss's door.

I heard the crash of splintered wood,
   The shouts of triumph, booted feet,
The crash of glass…
   A pistol shot rang out across
The silent street.

I rose; my pistol in my hand,
   I rose with sweat upon my palm
And hesitated, safe in darkness
   (that shot would surely raise alarm)
I listened to the brutal shout
   But dared not show my face without.
I heard her shriek, I heard her cry…
   I heard Joss shout, 'No! Let me die!'
I heard assault go on-and-on
   Beyond that pale and moonlit lawn,
And when they'd been –
   And when they'd gone
I sat and waited for the dawn,
   Sitting with my pistol drawn
Still cold within my clammy palm.
   Not having come to any harm
Re-lived again my moment of defiance;
   My act, my demonstration of reliance.

When all seemed calm
   And all seemed still
I'd crept up to my window-cill

   And with a bravely beating heart
Had watched the sated rebels part
   With haste, with stealth
And with a wealth
   Of backward glances
They set off at a trot.
   Then I had raised my pistol
With bravado for a shot.
   But fearful then of being seen
Ducked quickly back behind the screen
   And waited with the half-cocked gun
For Joss and Mrs. J to come.
   But all the while my waking dreams
Were filled with echoes of their
screams…

6.

Above the oleander as I crossed to Joss's lawn
   Streaks of light were breaking
Through the mist of early dawn.
   There was silence from the bungalow
Beyond the shattered door
   And glass and strips of curtain
Were scattered on the floor.
   I picked my way with stealth
Amongst the wreckage of their home
   And then I heard faint stirrings in the dark
And then a moan.

'I think I'll have another – you?
   Go on – a double – I will too.
Got no lemon I'm afraid
   But then we don't want lemonade.
Ha ha, we'll take it as it comes,
   (wish I could get this stuff in drums)
Not normally like this, you know,

But then – oh come on, don't be slow,
Where was I?
      Joss?
         Oh yes.
            Of course…'

7.

He was tied to a chair
  And from where
I stood
  I could see where they'd cut him,
The trickle of blood
  Flowing off the chair seat
Down his legs to his feet.
  And he looked at me – God –
With a sort of surprise
  And a - sort of a – queer look
Of shame in his eyes.
  Then he tilted his head, just a fraction,
No more
  To a bundle of blood-sodden rags
On the floor…

In that room
  In the gloom
Where my senses were reeling
  I stared at them both
With repression of feeling
  At Mrs. Joss dead,
Where he'd inclined his head,
  At the rug by the table
They'd used as a bed…
  And the blood at his feet
Flowing down from the seat,
  The murder of Joss
That they'd failed to complete;

And averting my eyes
From his look of surprise,
And with hands that were shaking
   And quivering thighs,
And crying and asking forgiveness in vain
   I shot him, and shot him, and shot him again.

8.

Oh God, like to have you here
   To hear my story, share a beer.
I think I need another gin
   Before I'm ready to turn in.

I left there shortly afterwards
   But no regrets, no that's no loss…
But had to leave it all behind
   (authorities were very kind)
But I remember Mrs. Joss
   Bloodstained muslin, tattered cotton,
Covered in a strip of lace
   But not enough to hide her face…..

6 THE WAR TO END WAR

Well – it didn't! What it did of course was to affect a fundamental shift in concepts from war as an honourable and glorious thing, to one of complete and utter indifference to the consequences for our fellow humans. The doctrine of 'the end justifies the means' was employed, where 'the end' (250 yards of barren mud) was entirely inconsequential while 'the means' were sacrificed on an obscene and grotesque scale.

As the guns fell silent the survivors fell silent too, waiting for the civilian babble to subside. Until slowly the truth and horror began to be revealed. No talk of hero's now. Only it mustn't happen again. And the glittering reputations of those who made brave decisions from beyond the range of shellfire on behalf of a million fellow humans began to be re-appraised.

Only, it mustn't happen again.

What a shame that a new generation could not learn the lesson bequeathed from the previous one which had suffered so much…

PALS

They said,
  'We'll all be pals together,
Charlie's going, so is Bert'
  We'll be in our own battalion…
Why does she look so hurt?
  She surely knows we have to
And I'm not the one to shirk
  When Lord K is calling for us
For a special kind of work.'

And he's so caught up in the fever,
  Impatiently waiting the day
To cast off his civvy boiler suit
  And take the army's pay.

Charlie's been round to say Sid's going too
  But Henry can't make it
(he's down with the 'flu)
  'Still he might catch up later –
Wont it be fun and together
  We'll all go and
Sort out the Hun.'

And she watched him with resentment
  As the days went swiftly by;
He couldn't wait to leave her
  (She tried hard not to cry).
The men were all like boys again,
  Her father just the same
As though they were off to an extra
  Special sort of football game.

But when at last the day came
  For them all to go away,
She was flushed with pride
  That she couldn't hide
As he marched so bravely from her side
  With flags and bands and bunting
(Oh! Wasn't it just a treat)
  Until they were passed
And she stood at last
  In the silent, empty street.

'They're gone,' she said to the echo
  As she turned towards their home.
'Gone,' it replied, 'swept on by the tide
  Of valour and honour and marshal pride.'
And she thought she heard his footsteps
  Returning down the street,
But the sound was drowned by the
  Pound Pound Pound of a million pairs of feet
As they followed the bugle
  And followed the drum and
The Sergeant Major's cry,
  Away to the gently flowing Somme
To die
  To die
    To die…

FREUNDEN

Far, far away it seemed,
  Oh, like something you had dreamed;
Muffled through the shaking ground,
  An eerie – sort of distant sound,
The British barrage falling round.

'That was a close one,' someone muttered
  As the shuttering creaked
And the lamp flame guttered
  And the streams of dust poured briefly down
In the gloomy dug-out underground.

The watch returned with some relief
  To the unit HQ far beneath
The parapet from where they'd been
  Behind their flimsy sandbag screen,
And told of all the things they'd seen
  (which wasn't much)
Just broken ground
  A few odd tree stumps scattered round
And drifting smoke, exploding shells,
  Cordite (and some other smell
On which it didn't pay to dwell).

And sometimes as the swirling smoke
  Drifted,
Lifted,
  Slowly broke,
They'd caught a glimpse, across the waste
  Of where the British line was placed
Before the smoke restored the screen,
  Obliterating what they'd seen,
Returning them to Dante's

Infernal dream of Hell.

So keep your head down, grit your teeth,
   You'll soon return to your friends beneath
(If you survive up here on the parapet
   And don't get hit, don't get hit...)

And if you do survive
   If you do come out alive,
You know what's coming don't you
   When they stop?
There's half-a-million Tommies
   Freshly waiting for the word
To attack when they swarm out
   Across the top.

So keep your head down Fritz
   When you're peering through the slitz,
All you have to do is to record their hitz,
   Record their hitz,
        Record their hitz,
Keep down low, keep down low,
   Record their hitz,
        Record their keep down low...

TEN THOUSAND EVERY DAY
(1972)

They gave the order eight miles back
   Along the sodden Northern track
Well out of sight and sound of flack
   And mortar bombs and tangled wire
And murderous machine-gun fire

And soldiers burning on the pyre
Of futile hope; and in the mire,
 Driven forward just like cattle
The last they heard – machine gun's rattle.
 Falling, dying where the stood
(and no-one knew quite why they should)
 I say – eight miles back from the blood
The general said, 'We'll take that wood.'

Calm and blue now, quite serene
 The sky,
Cloudless almost, arches loftily above
 The battlefield, indifferent to all the men
Who die.
 Bewildered and unthinking they
faithfully
Pass by,
 Stumbling dumbly on.
And all the birds have flown away
 From shellfire by both night and day.

For 'honour' and for 'glory' in the name
 Of 'God and King',
Because they caught the madness they
 Came out to 'do their thing',
And back across the Channel on the
 Music halls they sing
Of 'Blighty', 'Tipperary' and that
 Other hackneyed thing.
And nobody can guess the desperate
horror
 'till they bring
Home tens of thousands wounded
 In whose ears the guns still ring.
So on they go to Mametz Wood
 And nobody wonders if they should!

What did I see from where I stood?

I saw the land of the Somme as it lay
  Briefly silent
After the crash of bombardment.
  In the stunned stillness the ground ahead
Lay shattered.
  Where there had been grass and flowers
Was only broken earth,
  And of the scattered trees there was none
(for something else lay waiting on
  the Somme).

The stillness lasted moments and daringly
  A skylark flew
Until, back on the ground a whistle blew
  And the soldiers
In the trenches knew…
(But they didn't know as we do
  Who lay waiting on the Somme).
The noise of battle rises to a crescendo as
  He stirs, rises and with a mighty flourish
Darts gleefully amongst the armies
  On the plain
And His great scythe sweeps back and forth
  Again…
           Again…
                      Again…
And as the soldiers fall and die
  Death tallies up his score
Then
Whispers His dark secret in
  The generals' ear,
'Tomorrow and on every day
  Give me ten thousand more.'

THE OUTSIDER

I never cared about him then,
   When we were just kids in the street.
He never joined the gang
   To fool around and hang
About the lineside.
   We laughed, we swaggered
And thought ourselves superior;
   Taunting, poking fun.
He was an outsider.

Well, he went to be a clerk
   (With his starch collar and airs)
While we went to the foundries along
   The riverbank, to a hooting
Hammering, steam blasted,
   Coal-fired, sweaty, swearing
Loss of innocence among the men.
   And we thought him soft.

Then I saw him in the ranks
   (with his pips)
Along with other men from banks
   And brokers' houses, among
Comrades of his own. I raised
   My head but he turned instead
Back to the men of his platoon.
   Always knew he was stuck-up.

Until the last time I saw him.
   Left, along the line, walking
Like the rest - in time –
   Just as we had all been drilled
To do.

   Two hundred, line abreast, but
Thinning, always thinning.
   But I'm still here, and over to the left
So is he.
   The tall summer grasses shimmer into dust
Under the flail of the guns
   But he,
      Like me,
           Marches steadily on until
Charmed, he reaches the line
   His young face innocent with endeavour.
And they rose before him – three – and
   Plunged their bayonets in.
No wonder he didn't want
   To join our gang..

THE TEARS OF AUTUMN

The simple people came,
   The simple people came;
They stood in the tears of autumn
   In the thin November rain,
With the sombre drum
   And the sombre flag
And the sombre thin parade
   Whilst memories tinged with glory
Rose as memorial wreaths
   Were laid.

Briefly now and briefly,
   And stepping slow and slow
They marched in comradeship again

As they had so long ago.
And the gentle tears of of autumn
   Fell unceasing as they stood,
Recalling fallen comrades
   (forgetting all the blood)

Just
   'Charlie, died a hero.'
And
   'In memory of our Bert,
Dead
   But not forgotten.'
And we'll put aside the hurt
   For they're heroes, yes they're heroes,
And that's how we'll recall
   As the gentle tears of autumn
In November start to fall.

A REPUTATION
(Required to fall)

I saw him twenty years ago
   Through the smoke
Through the haze,
   Exactly as it must have been
(the tale that he's recounting)
   To the group's admiring gaze.

He was
   Replete with – well – dainty fare
But plenty; choice cuts, puddings,
   A piquant sauce,
The tradition of the port (of course…)

The evening transmutes from food
To recollection.
  A lugubrious tale
With which to regale them
  From the high Board,
Verbiage follows roughage
  As an aid to digestion.

There's florid laughter, careless
  Of the victims of the tale
Told so well, heard before,
  Always a pleasure.
'Well,' a rustle of suppressed amusement,
  'There they were d'you see…'
From supercilious uncaring brutes
  Come echoes in my mind
Of that guffaw
  And the disconnected face bathed
In admiration of his peers. Glowing
  Through cigar smoke I see him
Down the years, flushed with excess,
  Flushed with memory of success.

Only –
  It wasn't success at all
Considering those who,
  Because they knew
No better,
  'Jumped to it,'
When he was about,
  Urged on by someone else's shout
While he passed by
  With condescending eye
Indifferent
  So long as they were good enough.
All they were worth to him,

    Two pence a dozen
(Not pay! No, the price
  Of a cartridge for a gun,
What it cost
  To stop their dreams
        Forever).

And now
  I see him again
In his dotage,
  Bloated,
Florid and replete
  With life,
Deep in his seat,
  A rug, a cushion
For his feet,
  Ready to repeat
Through memory's magnifying eye,
  'the way it was, d'you see…'
Coloured by brandy,
  Success re-lived
Only – I repeat,
  It wasn't success at all
When
  For one questionable reputation
So many others
  Were required to fall.

7   A FINAL SOLUTION

We are still trying to come to terms with it. The Holocaust. True understanding will never come because we as individuals – you and I – could never bring ourselves to do such a thing and would never tolerate such a state of affairs. We are civilised.

So was Germany. In fact Germany was no less civilised than the rest of Europe, and perhaps better than most. But the paradox is clear; we would not tolerate such a thing and it is that very intolerance which enabled the German people to be deceived into tolerating the Final Solution. The question of morality, of pity, of right or wrong simply did not exist. And now we have the example in history of just how far we can go as individuals, or collectively, or as a nation state.

Individuals may be punished but the punishment can never match the enormity of the crime. And how do you punish a nation? And why should that nation's new-born children suffer for the sins of the parents?

The present offers no explanations of the past but it does pose the uncomfortable question regarding how – by a strange quirk of human nature – the victims themselves became accomplices.

THE BRIEF ILLUSION
(1982)

You stood with those other shuffling
   Ruined creatures and watched him go.
Didn't you!

And took a sort of consolation.
   Didn't you!

Saying,
   'Is it for the best?
Oh yes it must be so.'
   And closing your eyes and
Closing your mind
   To the bittersweet closing of the door
Through which he passed.
   Then looking around you in despair,
Hopeless,
         Hopeless,

Saying,
   'Farewell oh my dear son
Farewell, the pain is sharp
   And cuts so deep
But in an instant you'll
   Be in the peace
Of eternal sleep,
   Restored once more
To the warming sunshine and light
   Of life beyond...'

And there was no crying as you
   Watched him go, herded away
Like so much cattle with the others,
   The batch for today.

But you stood by the wire
  Ashamed,
        Ashamed,

Asking,
  'How can we be so far removed
From the happiness
  And golden times of sweet Bohemia?
Barefoot and free along the banks
  Of our brightly tumbling stream,
Hard against the forest,
  Where we washed our weary
Feet of the sun-warmed earth
  And watched fish gliding swiftly
In the cool, cool, flow.'

Such tales they told.
  They said that we
Through labour could become
  Quite free,
And brought us here.
  Whatever should we fear?
Why? – because it is a dark and dismal
  Place of eternal winter,
Unrelieved by the slightest spark
  Of warmth or pity,
Oppressed and forever dominated by those
  Five grim and busy chimneys.

One in so many…
  Day after ceaseless day…

Why, my son it can only be
  Just a twinkling of light away
That's all.

Sleep on,
Sleep on forever in my memory...

Did they do as you had hoped?
　Did the sharp
Cutting breath of gas
　Sever in a flash
That golden thread of life?
　Was he gone without fear
With only the thought of you
　He held so dear?
Did he leave with
　A final act of compassion?

Should I tell?
　And if I do will your soul burst forth
Crying to the eternal heaven
　'No! No!'
Shrieking and lost in madness?

Will you picture the prick of a needle
　So judiciously applied?
Or a rifle-butt
　So cleverly put
That he sank to the floor and cried?
　Or the care they took to restore him
And the hope that he nursed of release,
　'till they took him again
And drove him insane
　With knives and with needles
And terror and pain?

And shall I relate
　How long was the wait
Until he passed out
　From the mortuary gate,

So many days after
   You bid him farewell
Without a tear?
   Or would you prefer not to hear
But to nurse your final
   Brief illusion?

THE VANISHING
(Not to give offence)

THEM
Thousands passed this way.
   Made to stand
In line behind the mound,
   Listening to the gunshots from
The far side of the ground.
   Unable to give comfort.
Or receive.
   Then – in twenties- climb
Down the crude steps in the wall,
   Scrambling onto the obscene floor,
Made to lie -
   'Closer! Closer!' -
Upon its nakedness.

HIM
God this is a boring job. I'll have a fag.
   'Come on you lazy swines – bring 'em up!'
Load the gun again. Be here all bloody day!
   Haven't we got a drink
Or something to keep us going?
   That's it, another magazine in. 'Stand clear.'

Dammit, dropped me fag.

ME
I will not protest.
  For in the inevitable march of time
Each moment is precious.
  To place my hand upon her head, the dark
Curling hair (it caught the sunlight
  Even there.)
No time for shame – I take her hand
  As it shakes and she looks…
Just looks…
  Saying nothing by word or hidden glance
But stands
  Naked
        And close,
            Waiting…

NOW
The queue moves forward. Twenty more.
  Politely and brisk
So as not to give offence
  Scrambling down the worn-earth steps,
Helping children, stumbling
  Over bodies – a freshly soft and yielding
Floor beneath the idle
  Swinging boot.
He sits, smoking, his gun at rest.
  'Closer!'
This close?
  'Lay down!'
But where is…? Where is Anna?
  Never mind, not to give offence…
And the world vanished in a gunshot.

VICTORY MARCH OF '45
(1985)

Victory! Victory! The scent is in the air,
   Like baying hounds who've run to ground
Their quarry to his lair.
   Borne on by irresistible momentum to pursue
Our enemy,
   Who melts away before us like the dew.
We harry them and hurry them
   Across the fields of spring,
(They must know they're defeated
   That they're trapped within a ring).
Our armour and our infantry
   Relentlessly advance;
Before us our adversary,
   Bewildered, in a trance.

The battle (what an understatement)
   Penetrates the Reich.
Elated we push onward to
   Prepare the final strike,
And on, and on and on, and on...
   Eagerly on to keep up and catch up
The German army, whose resistance
   Before us
Becomes less and less
   Until we realise
The open country
   Ahead
Is free
   As far as our eyes
And our spies
   Can see.

So onward and blindly, onward we go.
   To left and to right is no sign of the foe.
(Has he gone and surrendered,
   The old so-and-so?)
Through woodland and ditches
   And meadows and farms,
Through uncanny silence
   (No sounds or alarms)
And the countryside stealthily
   Loses its charms.

But none of us noticed that.

Continuing on our headlong way
   Elating thoughts of victory
Coming closer day-by-day
   On we sped.
Retribution (we anticipated)
   Lay ahead.

Remember, remember
   Just a few short weeks ago
How heroically and lustily
   Cheering we marched through
Newly liberated towns
   And received their wild acclaim,
All their joyous adulation;
   It was everywhere
The same.
   Brief delirium, like gods.
And then we rumbled on again.

The remembering makes me pause
   And look about the too quiet countryside
Happy in the sun.

Am I alone in sensing quiet, solitude...?
'To hell with it! – Come on, get on!'
And so we do, plunging on headlong
In triumph.

Ahead of us lay a barracks.
  Our brisk approach slowed
And nearer, we stared,
  Aghast and horrified
At our inheritance.

Oh pity me for seeing what I do.
  And pity them
Who also stare
  Without emotion at our approach.
What can I say to you?
  For words cannot replace lost souls,
Lost years, and lives and loves
  Destroyed within this grey and rotting
place.
And pity is not enough,
  And emotions can never reach the depth
of
Compassion which you feel.
  And so – strangely – you feel nothing,
And you look at your companions
  And see that they too are suffering
From a sudden repression of emotion.
  And then you know that this is real as
You pick your way carefully
  Into the fragile life and wonder,
'Where do I start?'

Are you ashamed of
  Your helplessness faced with
Such desperate need?

Are you ashamed? –
Of your revulsion as
   They brush against you?
Are you ashamed
   Of your desire to run
And not look back?

Oh God! God! These are the innocents.
   Thousand upon thousand.
In dying need..
   Of something…
And they don't know what it is!
   And for a long time (God help you)
Neither do you.
   But your headlong flight is stopped
Right there
   And your triumph melts
Into the air
   And quietly you stand,
And quietly you stare…

THE DENTIST
(My earliest surviving poem – in blank verse!)
(1959)

I lay in a deep, sublime, dark flowing
   Pool of sleep.
Unconscious, unaware for all I know
   (And yet we have no recollection
That will show
   The state of our well-being when we fall
Deep in the arms of slumber).
   Yet I repeat, my rest I supposed

To be
   Complete.

But reluctantly I emerged…

   Through swirling mist which thinned, gave way
Re-clouded over 'till
   With the intensity of hot day's sun
It was gone.

I know I slept yet here I was, awake
   In a great sand arena,
A sunken pit, a lake
   Of sand with marble sides
Garlanded with wreaths.
   And an all-embracing murmur of low
noise
Came from ten thousand blurred and
moving
   Image faces jostling in their seats
To gaze upon the days' delights.

I gazed about, amazed,
   I seemed to know the place.
My companions in this pit
   Were strange to me,
Not one I knew and yet…
   And yet…

We strayed into the centre, away from
   The festooned marble sides;
Despite the heat staying close, one against
   The other, sweating in frightful
anticipation.
And shuffling softly on the sand, drifting
   Like an uneasy herd we waited until

An emperor, purple robed,
   Took his place above.

Am emperor with lofty gaze, brows
   Bound with golden leaves
And flanking, either side, Praetorians
   Black armed who looked down
With sneering eyes
   Upon the crowd
Whom they despised.
What did we here?
   What role, what part had we to play?
My rising unease turned to fear,
   Transmitted by the fear of those around.
The sun climbed higher still and
   Poured its withering heat direct
Upon the ground,
   Into the dazzling arena where we
Stood bewildered and afraid.
   Way out? – we knew of no way out
At all.
   The only way was in, through barred
gates
Set round the area wall,
   Each now guarded.

The hungry multitude above, the crowds
   Remained the same,
A murmuring ebb and flow of sound
   Along the lofty terraces but now
Charged with tension, a strange
   Exhilaration that foretold of
Imminent desperate things to come.
   I looked at my companions and felt
The same
   Fearful anticipation. A few unable to

Sustain their nerve sank kneeling to the
ground
   And prayed, murmuring
Your Name.

The emperor had made a sign.
   We didn't see but felt a change
Alive in the air and then?
   No appeal. Resign, accept
What has to be.
   What is this total calmness that descends
On him, on them, on me?
   And now we raised our eyes and gazed
Without emotion
   To where the gates within the marble
walls
Were open.

And emerging armed guards, soldiers who
   Fanned out in neat precision
Encircling our poor defenceless band.
   We looked about, seeking some place
To go;
   This cannot please, this cannot be so
soon
The end.
   The sun beat down upon the pure white
Marble beauty of the place; banners hung
   And fluttered in the breeze,
A range of contradicting perfumes entered
   My heightened senses.
Too late!
   Too late!
With steadfast march the black-robed
guards
   Were upon us with swords upraised

And while we ran and scattered plunged
patiently
  After us, despatching one-by-one
All to the crowd's
  Enthusiastic cheer.
Running, stumbling, thinning and still
  They came leaving my late companions
Bodies on the sand.
  I turned and ran.
Then turned, could run no more. And on
  He came. I stood and watched in fear
As on he came…
  The arena still was white
    The sun was bright
      My skin was warm
        My eyes shed tears
          He raised his dripping sword
            I fell onto my knees and
Cried
    And cried…
          And as I cried…

… the echo of my voice died
  In the frosty air;
Only my whisp of breath hung softly
there.

I stared and gaped in disbelief,
  Shuddering in the creeping, clammy
cold,
With people all around me dressed in rags
  With hollow eyes in faces young and
old.
Festooned in dirt some stood, shuffling
  With rags upon their feet.
Outside the wind whipped up the snow,

Inside the filthy shed no light, no heat.
The children white with hunger,
　Thin and cold clung, frightened
And took hold
Of mothers' skirt,
　The sleeve of fathers' shirt,
Crawling close for safety in the dirt.
　Whilst others sat in groups with empty eyes
And made no sound save moans
　And doleful sighs,
Whilst here and there a sickly baby cries.

We look and stiffen. From without
　We hear a muffled, rasping shout,
A row of muffled boots upon the snow,
　The door flings open and
We are surveyed with bored indifference
　By an officer; from polished boots
And pistol belt to cap
　His uniform, like death, completely black
Bearing deaths emblem.

Am I here?
　I witness all the scene and yet remain
Immune from all that follows.

They enter, great-coated and file out
　Heel to heel with pistols drawn,
Shooting into the poor defenceless crowd,
　Advancing to pick their dainty way between
The dying and the dead, pointing
　Their deliberate pistols where they lie,
Going back for those they miss whilst
　In their wake amongst the bloody

Broken faces comes
   The dentist
In deaths head black just like the rest
   Who carries out his duty,
Does his best,
   Probing the gaping mouths he
Draws the teeth, seeking their gold
   He probes and fills his bulging bag
And leaves them in their mutilation…
   What fearful scenes to haunt the mind,
What fearful acts of men against
Mankind.

RETURN TO ROMANCE

The romance of life, of love and the fortune of war.

EN FAMILLE

HANDS

Why is you hand so soft in mine.
Your hand so soft and strong?
Your hand I cover with mine own
Yet yours leads mine along.

THE DOUBTER 'IF'
(To Judy on joining me at threescore and ten)

If I could start again
To love again,
Just as I did
The day I lost my heart…

If I could swoon,
Captured in the radiance
Of your smile, beneath the moon,
That pierced my heart…

If I could feel those
Memories in my mind,
As real as on those days
We left behind…

Where joy resides with love
That doubter 'if'
Can hold no sway,
For when I see
Your look,

> Your smile on me,
> I feel the way
> I used to feel,
> Today.

TO MY LOVE
(1977)

There's a moon that brightly gleams
>> Beyond the drifting clouds,
And the soft and balmy breeze
>> Gently whispers from the trees
As the dark road
>> Welcomes away into the night.

In the shadow of a wall they stand,
>> He with his arms about
The lady that he loves, content
>> Within their youthful world.
Murmuring their devotion
>> And oblivious to me…

Do you remember days when we
>> Kept similar trysts 'neath similar trees
So many light summers ago
>> In dark velvet moonlight,
The dark fanning breeze?

I am oppressed by intimations of mortality,
>> For how much happiness
Can a man deserve.?
>> I've lived with you and loved with you
So many, many years

Whilst all around the world is blessed
            With sorrow and with tears.
But our children lie their golden heads
            In sweet content upon their beds
With angels there to keep
            Them safely in their sleep.

Kiss them softly for me as I kiss you now.
            Hold their hands, stand with them
In the sun. Wherever I may be
            You will always be with me
And I shall always be upon my journey home.
            For home is where the heart is
And you hold my heart in your look
            And in your touch.
The heart of my heart resides with you –
            Nurse me gently so that I may return.

HEARTSEASE
(1992)

Heartsease. Sitting by the fire
Remembering
    The things we used to do
           Together,
    Me and you.

Heartsease. All the time
           Your hand in mine,
    Walking, talking,
           River white with blossom in the sun;
    Water meadows
           In the rain.

Sheltering,
> Sunshine,
>> Home again.

Heartsease. Memories sustain
> The spirit,
Ease the pain
> Of loneliness.
You're never really gone;
> Memories
Can almost bring you back again…

Heartsease.
> Embers of
A dying flame.

G.W.C.'
(For Judith – a daughter's tribute)

And through my life
  The one you gave to me
I will know you again in memory;
  Sublime and happy days
Recaptured without pain.

These are the places
  Where we came.
And, where happiness waits
  We come again.
A happiness of which so much was due,
  Not false, contrived with artifice,
But to your simple presence -
  You.
Content, within your time;
  A friend secure within

Your friendships.
   We laughed and you laughed too -
I hear it carried in the wind,
   Chiming with the merriment of children,
Amused at the foibles of your self.
   But never changing, never
Of conscious will
   And always content to be still
The governor of our time.

Upon the cliff, we look below
   And see you on the bay
Still and in content,
   A quiet man.
Here, the same wind carries
Time borne images across the bay
   To here, your resting place,
A place of smiles and laughter.
   Silent now.
The sigh of wind fanned grass,
   And distant childhood,
A lapping wave upon the shore.
   Wind borne and free,
Swirling softly into your haven
   And falling gently, gently to the sea.

THE THIEF WHO COMES IN THE NIGHT
(A memoriam for Margaret Carter, nee Greenfield)
(1978)

Who will return her love to thee
Now that she is gone? – stolen
Away by that thief who comes in the night?

Who can restore the happiness
    Once shared – those innocent
Simple pleasures that drew
    Two loving hearts together?

Now only memories remain of sunlit
    Days; of cornfields full
Of poppies, and the scent of lilac
    Drifting across the lawn,
And you, and he
    (the thief who comes in the night).

And who will erase the hurt we shared
    With you
When once we knew
    That with silent, stealthy feet
The thief had been in the dark
    Of our ignorance
And left his mark.

Oh, what can we do? And why
    Should he have chosen you.
Why does he make you waste away
    And die so slow,
This dreadful thief who visits us at night?

HOW CAN YOU CRY?
(1976)

A sad and shallow vale of tears
  Is what this life, to some, appears
With sadness marring fun and joy
  Our own misgivings thus destroy
The way in which we ought to cope
  And come through life, eyes bright
With hope.

So sit with me and you will see
  A rare woodpecker on a tree;
The apple blossom, pink and bright;
  Two noisy sparrows in a fight.
When such sweet sorrows fill your day
  How can you cry your life away?

AUGUST 11 1977

I came to see you yesterday.
  Did you know?
I stood in the sunshine of the still
  Warm evening
At the place where you lie in dignity
  And tried to capture the fabric of
My memories.
  As easy might I capture the wind.

Oh! but you have peace,
  There on the hillside beneath the yew.

Only the hum of the bees and the faraway
  Call of the dove where
The summer air blows
  From the distant Malverns.
Just I, in the stillness, in the sun
  With my memories,
      And you…

HOW MANY HOURS…?

How many hours did we sit beside…?
Exchanging looks we couldn't hide,
In silence?
Willing the love
Like a thread of light
Between us,
Dancing across the boundless chasm of
Understanding.
Me and you;
You and I,
In the long, slow, ticking seconds of time,
Welding our lives together,
Bridging boundaries and belief,
All consumed in one blinding, lingering,
How-long look between us.

How many hours
Ago…?
Not hours now but years. I know
Age withers and demeans
But there is still that instant hour
Of dreams,
When young eyes meet;

The yawning chasm told in years,
Disappears,
And your bright young eyes of love meet
Mine with smiles.

FOR JUDE
(The secret life)

The days of my life are shrouded in time
And the sweet joys of manhood,
Renewed in my prime
   Are fleetingly precious to me.
And the joy of your happiness shows
   In your smile
As you linger, content, in my arms for a while.

So here's to the secret, our life of shared love,
   And the fever that mounts as we lay,
Of delight in the pleasures, oblivious to care,
   A lifetime of loving with passion we share.

Oh! wanton, you woman, oh! wanton my wife,
   So tender, so breathless and lustful, so soon
This hour will not end, nor this afternoon
   Until we fall back with love's requited swoon.

The living mem'ries are the same,
The way we were, and still remain.
Though years may pass no minute's lost
When love is given reckless reign
To tender love's desire insane!

Oh sweet oblivion in your arms,
We think we'll never feel again.

I see it now within your eyes
The love, the lust shorn of disguise;
The invitation to your thighs.

And seeing you, in memory,
The way we thought we used to be,
My mind reveals, my senses reeling
   Not shadows lost - but renewed feeling.
Your eyes invite me to begin.
   And oh! the softness of your skin.
Forget the cleaning, shopping, cooking
   Let others be the slaves of clock;
Don't be afraid of others looking
   Let them sneer, let them mock,
Reject all care; my heart is beating!
   A gift so rare should not be fleeting,
Hurried, or subsumed with guilt;
   Our life's renewed beneath the quilt;
Come, let's enjoy it to the hilt.

UPON MEMORY'S WINGS
(for Judy's father, GWC)

Above the spangled, waveless sea,
   Washed by delighted infant laughter,
Here where the air hangs
   Still and fragrant, heavy
On the flowered grasses
   Was where the vigil was observed.
So briefly.

But in the immemorial cries
   Of children,
In the endless sound of lapping water,

In the stillness beyond distant sounds
That brevity was timeless.

A life encompassed,
  Moments instantly recalled
And laid to rest,
  Leaving the savour
Of his pleasure,
  A simple memory
As overlaid as tapestry,
  Within our mind he lives,
Complete.

Each grain takes the
  Briefly soaring memory,
Fragmented and dispersed
  Amongst the joyous life below,
Spreading, like his goodness always was,
  Amongst his fellow men.

FLUTTERBY
(For Julia, 3)

Summer breezes gently sigh
  Under cloudless sunlit sky;
And if you should cast your eye
  You might see a butterfly
            Flutterby.

Where the happy garden showers
  All our senses through the hours
With the scent and sight of flowers,
  Just for this white butterfly
            To flutterby.

GOD – THE FATHER

And it came to me sharp as a pin
That I knew who was meant to be Him;
For the father of childhood I followed with love
Gave me love in return, like it came from above.
For in childhood from birth until I was seven
He was God incarnated on Earth, not in heaven
Who, regarded in awe through my innocent eyes
Was majestic, omnipotent, loving and wise.
And I treasured his footsteps as homeward
We trod
Knowing God is the Father, the father is God.

LOVE SANS HOPE

Little boy who made thee?
  Dost thou know who made thee?
T'was thy father on this Earth,
  He's the one who gave thee birth,
Took away thy mother's mirth,
  He's the one who made thee.

Little boy show honour
  Tio that man, thy father.
For he suffered and knew loss,
  Like the Saviour on the cross
Much to his – and thine own cost –
  He thou should'st now honour.

Little boy he loved thee.
  Don't deny, thou must see.
All he sought was love returned
  While the love for which he yearned,

Like his hopes was shattered, burned.
   He's the one who loved thee.

Where's the love that bound thee?
   That used to surround thee?
If thou knowest thou must say.
   'T'was fierce, possessive, fed by grief.
Which denies love and belief.
   Like the waning of the day
Of childhood, filled with play,
   Love sans hope refused to stay.'

WHAT'S IN A NAME?

What's in a name?
   Four letters to describe a boy?
Impossible!

But joy and wisdom fills his eyes
   Now he is five.
A universe of knowledge unfolding
   In his play;
The innocence with which he fills
   Each day.
The happiness he so freely
   Gives away.
Heaven is in his name,
   The taste of childhood's summer fruit;
Jack, my yesterday.

MY LITTLE DAUGHTER

I love my little daughter,
  I love to see her hair.
It cascades just like water,
  It's long and wavy, fair.
She comes along to tell me things,
  All serious and true,
And gazes with an earnest gaze
  From eyes of cornflower blue.

And as she tells me I pretend
  That I've misunderstood.
She looks at me in retribution
  (Well you know she would).

And 'cos she knows that I was kidding,
  That it's just a game
She wags her finger, ticks me off
  But loves me just the same.

MY SON (THE GREAT TEENAGER)

'Hi dad..!'
  His greeting, casual above
The thud of music
  Meets me on the threshold
And I'm home.
  The golden sunlight of his voice.

THE COLOURS

Without my love, my friend, my wife,
    These other two would not have life.
And what a place the world would be
    Devoid of all the things we see;
The things we do, the things we share,
    The simple act of 'being there'.
Without my love, my friend my wife
    There'd be no colours in my life.

J'ACCUSE

OZYMANDIAS AGAIN

Feed music to me,
    Notes and vision
And release it upon the air.
    Send the excitement and
The peace of symphony upon
    Its final glorious way, for
The tiny men are bent upon
    A last farewell.

There is a rose,
    Heavy with musky scent,
Bright and oh! so beautiful
    Against the darkness of the leaf.
Heavy with peace and leisure
    The mystic scent of flowers
Opens up the senses

      And defies the tiny men
Whose wisdom is measured on a miniscale.

Consider –
      'I can pluck a skylark
From the sky (who knew no wrong
      But soared and warbled clear and high)
And whisk him clear away.'

'And I can still
      The pure and mighty voice
Of music indeed I can –
      Starting with a mighty BANG
Continuing with the
      Wail and mourn of endless
Suffering and disease.
      For I am Man;
Mighty and all-powerful.
      FEAR ME!'

Would you dare to do all this?
      Fear? – I pity you,
You dwarf of tiny intellect
      Who knows not how to create,
And must
      Therefore
            Destroy.

THE LOST SOULS

Beyond darkness!
      What lies beyond the all-embracing
dark?
Nothing.

    No perception nor way to see,
No depth, no way ahead.
    Sole consciousness; alone.
Only
    Dread anticipation of
Unknown..?

Held close, rigid, frozen in mobility,
    Drifting in the void
Of ignorance
    And fear.
What lies in the darkness?

There is a distant sense of presence,
    Faint echo of a cry,
The dreamlike chaos
    Of a myriad wandering souls
Lost in the oblivion of
    Newborn ignorance.

The sense of presence
    Drawing close,
Drifting current eddies,
    An approach,
Search, a touch,
    Soft and suddenly withdrawn
And screaming
    As the eddies swirl, and
Shrieking rises in
    The unseen multitude
'till panic subsides
    And the waves recede
To leave
    You tumbling
Slowly through the sense-less void.
    Again.

'Hear me,' said the spirit,
    'hear me and listen.'
And again a ripple passed
    Through them
As they turned, writhing, straining
    Peering sightless into
Darkness. And they perceived...?
    Nothing.
Save utter black.
    Despairing.

'Hear me.' Again a gentle wave
    Of hope ran through eternity.
Again they strove
    And peered and lurched,
Questing for - ?
    They knew not what.

'I am here.'
    The fury of despair increased,
A storm of anguish deep
    In the eternal well of darkness.
And the voice ceased,
    The spirit
Withdrew;
    Wild lamentation grew.
All save one
    Who looked instead
Within,
    With closed unseeing eyes.
And the furious storm receded
    In his presence as he whispered,
On the wave,
    'I hear.'
And the voice replied, 'Open up your heart,

    Do not search; I will come
To you.
    Know only I am with you.'
But the man raised his eyes to see
    A revelation, of light
Breaking on the darkness.
    And searched for the spirit source –
But it was gone, lost
    In the darkness as before.
And he returned to the despairing world
    Of emptiness and lost souls,
Adrift upon the void…

THE RIGHTS OF MAN

Dreams of heroism, service
Filled the child horizon of the man;
Forthright and eager with ramrod back,
The smartly snapped salute – turn –
And march in faultless step. The dream
    Became reality.

At which the other scoffed,
    At the aspiration of
The brother. Whilst he, in indolence
Pursued his shameful indulgence.

Life brough diverse rewards.
Imprisonment, disgrace
For the brother on the take.
For the first, the call to arms
Brought Glory in its wake.
But – imprisoned; sheltered, warm
    The lesser one was fed

Whilst sacrificed, the noble one lay
Mutilated, dead.

EVERMAN'S CHILD
(A Press photo of a child in India, condemned to die for being mentally ill)

Where is she now, this child of mine,
  With eyes demure and the smile divine
And the spirit so free,
  Who meant nothing to me?

Her innocent mind was unsullied and kind
  And trusting and pure, direct and demure
And so unlike me.
  She means nothing you see.

She's just wanting and needing, and
  In between feeding
Just stays in her place
  With that look on her face
Unaware of the shame
  That she brings to my name.

And it isn't just pity the people express
  As they towel her clean, and clean up
The mess;
  There's fear and resentment that builds
In the crowd
  That between us we've let such a thing
Be allowed.
  So I did what I did,
        I abandoned the kid.

With a string for a collar she's tied to a tree
   And her home's in the squalor
Of faeces and pee
   In the ditch, and her nature, so sweet
Becomes twisted with torment
   Down there in the heat.

Beyond understanding the people pass wide,
   Unlooking, unloving,
        Not caring, nor staring,
   Nor heeding, nor feeding
        Nor washing nor cleaning,
Ignoring the cries of her wailing and keening.
   And the eyes so demure, and the smile
So divine
   Fade slow in the terrible passage of time
'till she dies.
   No-one cries.

THIS IS THE WAY OF MODERN MAN

This is the way that modern man
   Resolves disputes, because he can.
      As in Iraq so with Iran.
Tho' Russia failed in a ten-year war
   As yanks did twenty years, before
They were kicked out from Vietnam
   As Russia was in Afghanistan,
This is the way of modern man.

This is the way we create furore
   With lies just as they lied before
(on some pretext
   To target the next)

'There's no alternative,' he swore,
  'Reluctantly we go to war.'
And lies lie soft beside the deceit
  Of millions who protest in the street.

Now a lesson must be learned
  And a lesson must be taught,
Freedom has to be conferred
  (Ask – at what price was it bought?)
Integrity that once we treasured,
  Honour that was once our pride
Can no longer now be measured
  When cynically its cast aside.

THE IRISH FUSILIER
(1985)

'Oi've been hit!' he exclaimed
  In a voice like he meant
That the last threepenny piece that he owned
  Had been spent.
'Oh lord, tell me mother…'
  He exclaimed as he stood,
And tasting the hot,
  Salty sweetness of blood
He stumbled and swayed
  And lay dead in the mud.

AND GOD CREATED...?
(On the creation of a living, artificial life cell)

It had a life but had no soul,
  It was complete but wasn't whole.
I felt its eyes surveying me,
  It scrutinised but couldn't see
Beyond the image, to my soul;
  For I am man, and I am whole.

I reason, not just calculate,
  I love and cherish – and I hate.
My certitude, alloyed with doubt
  Gives me – and others – a way out.
The gulf 'twixt reason and insane
  Gives me a mind, not just a brain.

Now doubt comes rushing with a roar;
  I know not what the robot's for!
It cannot care, it cannot love,
  It does not have the power to move
With argument and sweet persuasion
  The passions of a living Nation.

Cold, inanimate, uncaring,
  Devoid of charity or sharing,
It lives, malignant in its box,
  Secure – we think – with bars and locks.
But those who started on the quest,
  Who denied doubt, thought they knew best
And thought they could create a brain
  Will wish they could begin again.

For what is made can't be unmade,
  And life-force cannot be enslaved.

And evolution, warped and twisted,
   Will still evolve, won't be resisted,
And subjugated, poor mankind
   By science will be left behind.

And human history will falter
   On blind reason's care-less altar,
Humiliated and oppressed,
   Ignored…
        Exploited…
                Laid to rest…

THE HISTORY OF NAPALM
(A naked Vietnamese child running up a road screaming in pain)

The history of napalm is really quite a scream,
   Its quite unlike the old flame gun
With burning kerosene.
   No, napalm is the product of
A new perverted dream.

It doesn't work on buildings, on bridges
   Or on roads;
It's not the force of detonation
   As the thing explodes
That makes it so effective –
   No, it's unlike all of those.

Its just a burning jelly – it's for people
   Do you see?
And where it hits is where it sticks,
   Indiscriminately.
And melts the skin through flesh to bone.
   Hmmm…!

But people will find ways to cope;
  You cannot stifle human hope.
So scrape it off, ignore the pain
  Perhaps the skin will grow again.

But wait, what's this? a different smell?
  There's bonding agents in the gel!
So now it sticks. And burns like hell!
  It won't scrape off, it simply spreads
Hmmm.!
  We're going to need more Red Cross beds.

Hang on! – those crafty Vietnamese
  Have come up with another wheeze
To stop the napalm doing damage,
  They simply jump into the paddies
And, totally immersed in water
  They stop the burning and the slaughter.
Hmmm…! It's such a shame…

Hang on, there is a new solution
  To overcome this mass ablution;
Add phosphorous - it burns when wet!
  (That's the best we've thought of yet!)
That'll fox the crafty Viet.
  (I think….
Now what's a word that rhymes with army?
  Barmy?
Military – futility?
  Enemy – humanity?)
Hold on!
  Understanding – amphibious landing?
'Succour?' –
  'Nah, fuck her!'
        'Well… Thanks anyway…'

RETURN TO ROMANCE

ROMANCE

I had a dream, a golden dream
   Of chivalry.
Where all the land was fair, thriving
   Beneath the rule of an even
And tolerant hierarchy
   Of noble lords.
Who stood open and confident upon
   Their ground, surveying all
And saying,
   'This land is good.'
And people toiled to keep it so,
   Receiving just reward; with
Leisure, laughter and freedom.
   Where the seasons marched
Their steady way, from sowing time
   To harvest day
Through Christmas, that most
   Blessed time of year.
And the mighty rode forth to
   Defend the right in pride and justice
And where each, high or low, could call
   Upon his lord's obligation
For defence and succour against
   Oppression, lies and tyranny.

Was there ever such a golden land,
   Such an age as this? Bright
With colour to flatter and dazzle the eye?
   Where man-at-arms rode his destrier
Beside a placid, lily banked stream to

    Lofty towers high upon a crag?
  Was there ever such a place? And did not
    Men dream with high ideal of
Right for right and might for right
    And never low-born suffered
Wrong through poverty?
    Why 'Yes! Yes!' and 'Yes!' again.
Do your dreams not have origins?

THE KNIGHTOF NO RENOWN

There was mist upon the river,
    Life was stirring in the rushes
And cobwebs heavy with the dew
    Were hanging on the bushes,
And the moon was fading, waning
    In the last deep shade of night,
And the clouds, once limned in silver
    Blended formless, without light.

Away across the meadow
    Gently watered by the stream
All was silent in a candle-glow
    As distant as a dream,
In the chapel by the river,
    Still and silent as a ghost,
Which through all the hours of darkness
    To a stranger has been host.
And the mysteries of Paradise
    Were present in the air
For the demons of Beelzebub
    Have been confronted there.

The torments of the soul,
    Temptation and desire,
Arrogance and lofty pride
    The knight had faced and cast aside
Like insubstantial mist, a wraith
    Unable to withstand true Faith.
As the burning candle weakens
    And light begins to fade
And the Cross upon the alter
    Is retreating into shade,
The last assault of fiends and demons
    (poised to break the shield of Faith)
Rise and scuttle in the corners,
    Seek where weakness can be found
Reaching, groping from the shadows
    Stealthily across the ground…
The candle fails
    And dark prevails.

And so the knight yielding,
    On his knees kneeling,
Bows in submission
    To what e'ere may come,
The saints interceding
    (His terrors receding),
Hold demons at bay
    'till the dawn of the day.

For rising and breaking, the sun's beams
    Are raking and
Searching the church with a clear
    Crystal light;
Now stretching and yawning,
    Welcoming morning, his long vigil over
Rises the knight.

Rising from kneeling, cold and
    Unfeeling,
Facing the sunburst and bathed
    In its light,
Watching, surveying and
    All the while praying,
Raises spurs in his Left hand,
    The sword in his Right.

And he offers his blade and
    His Heart to the fight
For the poor and oppressed, to withstand
    Brutish might,
To be friend to the friendless and
    Fearing no fight
He awaits the priests Blessing
    This unhallowed knight.

As he waits at the altar
    His vows to fulfil,
Outside in the valley all's
    Quiet and still.
Not a sound, not a sparrow
    Has started to trill
As a horseman approaching
    Descends from the hill.

His armour is dull
    And his trappings are plain,
His destrier snorts, held back tight
    On the rein.
There is no insignia displayed on his chest,
    His helmet is plumed but
Carries no Crest,
    And armed with a lance,
A shield and a mace,

His visor is closed,
Concealing his face.

He walks his horse to the valley floor
    And beats upon the chapel door
Calling in tones that will not be denied
    'Come out Sir Knight,
Don't stay inside!
    Come out Sir Knight, for now is time
For us to settle at once the score!'
    And crying thus beats as before
With mailed fist upon the door.

The knight within with steady eyes
    Raised them upward to the skies
And listened to a voice which said,
    (as though a spirit in his head
Had taken his life to make it whole,
    Implanting Peace within his soul)
Words profound, which softly thrilled,
    'Your destiny is now fulfilled.'

So placing sword and spur
    Upon the altar there,
He walked to the door with measured tread
    To where the voice of Destiny led
And faced the mounted stranger,
    'Yes?'
And crossed himself like one who's Blessed.

The horseman looked down and gave answer,
    'Sir Knight you have denied my Master,
Which is something for which
    You must answer.
For having Vigil kept
    In search of Absolution

I have come to find you
        Seeking retribution.'
And he raised his lance
        With its point aloft,
Black pennant hanging in the still air
        And cast his gauntlet to the ground
Where it lay between them.

And the knight replied,
        'Know that I have done Homage
        Over my spurs
        But have not received the Blessing
        Nor the sacrament of Church.
And though I would not betray the vow
        Made here before the altar,
I must decline your challenge
        For fear of doing you dishonour.'

The stranger's mount pawed the ground,
        The stranger turned and
Gazed around,
        Then leaning forward softly said,
'By mid-day Sir
        I'll have your head,
For having prayed this night,
        And taken your knightly vow,
I am resolved Sir Knight
        That I will fight you now.
Take up my gage and face me,
        Dishonour is not mine,
For the vows you took in Holy Church
        You cannot now decline.'

So, kneeling, the knight
        Took up the gage
With unflinching gaze in a face so pale

  And returned to the chapel and
Knelt once more
  In prayer before the altar-rail.
'Seigneur you know I do not fear,
  For that is what has brought me here.
I will be chaste, I will be true
  For that is what I vowed to you.
But must my honour now be tested
  Before my Vows have been invested
With the Blessing in Thy Name?'
  And entering his mind there came
The voice – just as before – again.

'Sir knight – for thus you truly are –
  Now is the Earthly foe you face.
Your adversary travelled far
  To find this time, to find
This place.'

It wasn't fear that held him back,
  Nor was it weakness of resolve,
But doubt that he would prowess lack…
  'So soon, so soon,'
The doubt insisted, 'you and your
  Arms have not been blessed.
You're too untried, your arms untested
  For to enter this contest.'

Both conflicts now the Errant faced;
  To overcome without disgrace
Resolve the first, the next would follow,
  But fail and victory would be hollow.
'I will be Faithful, I'll be True.'
  He heard himself make soft reply.
'Fidelity I've sworn to You,
  Thus will I live, thus will I die.'

Beside the spurs placed on the altar
>He laid his sword, cast down his shield,
Went to the door and threw it open
>Calling upon his Foe to yield.

He saw the stranger urge him forward,
>Saw the stranger raise his mace,
'But no! the knight called from the chapel
>'I'll not fight there, 'tis no disgrace
But if you want my head from me
>Then you must do it in this place.'

'Then yes,' the stranger dismounted, roaring
>'Your ground or mine I'll not dispute.'
And leaving his great war-horse pawing
>He drew his sword and swung his mace
And rushed; the young knight stood his place
>And at the door his foe-man faltered,
Hesitated, took a pace then,
>False courage took its place.
He dropped his mace upon the sward,
>He took another step toward
And with both hands he raised his sword.

The knight stepped back,
>Into the shadow of Holy Church.
His foe pursued, but through the portal
>Stopped and staggered, gave a lurch.
The knight retreated to the altar,
>Raised his own sword, held it high;
The stranger, trying to pursue him
>Gave a most blood-curdling cry
Then hesitated once again
>And faltering, cried out in pain,
And looking at the sword in awe,

      Held like a cross in the young knight's hands
He fell and lay upon the floor
      And said, 'I make no more demands.
Do with me what you will, Sir Knight,
      For I am Temptation, sent against you
But here, within, I cannot fight.'

      The young knight knelt beside his foe
And said, 'You are forgiven – Go!'
      His sword, a crozier in the light
Fell like a cross in a shaft of sun,
      Its shadow covered the smile that grew
Over the face of Him that knew
      He need no longer to pursue
This purest Knight of No Renown
      Who would not fight, except with Faith,
And whispered, 'I die, and die unshriven.
      Only say I am forgiven.
For my quest is now complete,
      I lay your Victory at Your Feet.'
And the sun rose high on that hallowed place
      Amongst the Yew and the new-dug earth,
As the sword and spurs and
      The Stranger's mace
Were laid on the sod o'er
      The Stranger's face.
And the knight, thrice blessed
      Who had passed the test,
Mounted the hill, and turned at the crest,
      Raised an arm, saluted the Sun
And heard again the voice that said,
      'Be slow to condemn, be not false-led;
None are so pure as He who lays dead.'

THE GARDENER
(1976)

Grace and beauty, tolerance
        Good taste.
Simplicity of line and form,
        All things in their place.

What would you desire
        To bring fulfilment
To a life?
        A measure – some,
Perhaps not all -
        For circumventing strife?

At least appreciation
        Of another's needs.
(Consider me a gardener
        Simply planting seeds).

TO BEETHOVEN
(In gratitude)

We follow as a comet tail
  In your wake. Oh, the journeys
That we go upon!
  And whilst we can only peer about,
Amazed and overcome with
  Awe and wonderment at
The sights and sounds of your world
  You, who hear the voice of Divinity
And whose voyage is mapped

In the inspiration of its call;
Why, you travel upon your sublime way.
And the sweep of your achievement
Sucks along the lesser mortals
Such as we in your wake. Like Pilot
Fish feeding in gratitude from
The discard of the shark.
Mighty Beethoven, were you indeed
Divine, clothed in the frail and
Mortal raiment of a man?
And if we could hear your voices…
Oh, if only we could…

FAIRIES

Where do the Northern fairies live?
On the banks of tumbling stream
Overhung by bracken green
And thickly spreading, where the rocks
From broken, craggy upland moors
Tumble down.

And do they sometimes slyly peep
From tufted grass where rabbits, sheep
And curlews make their home?
Resentful when the city people
Careless, come to roam.

Who knows where they are?
Or if they still exist?
Or are they just an instinct, vague,
Lost in memory's mist?

THOSE SHOPPING DAYS
(1971)

Sheep and moorland,
  Granite crags;
Sheepskin, hopsack,
  Duffle bags;
Walking through the misty town,
  Splashing up and splashing down.
In and out the silly shops,
  Cheap perfume and malted hops.
Damn! Damn! Damn!

Weary head and weary heart,
  Waiting for the crowds to part,
Rubbing where your temples smart –
  Get the horse before the cart!
Running in and running out
  Of cash and inspiration.
Fin'lly elbowing like a lout
  In careless desperation.

Got to get the shopping done.
  Oh it should be much more fun.
Oh to Hell with everyone –
  MERRY CHRISTMAS!

LAMENTING THE MUSE
(1970)

Where has she gone, leaving only
  This sombre mood of melancholy?
Why, the sun still shines as brightly
  This high summer day, whilst the
Languid breeze blows gently through
  The trees.
The garden, just as bright with
  Flowers as before.
So why do I regard it with so much
  Distaste?
Away from this tumbling world. You
  Can grub around amongst yourselves
Like pigs for all I care. You stink
  With the vomit of commerce. We
Should be away you and I, where the
  Breeze blows fresh and clean from
The far, far ocean and only the
  Gulls cry, wheeling high
Around their lofty cliffs, and woodsmoke
  Drifts across the broken shore.
Beyond the foam, beyond the far horizon,
  A distant dream of home.

TRAFALGAR MORNING
(1970)

Cold and damp the grey
  October day.
Dawning soft on the gently swelling sea
  The rising sun, hidden by close sea-mist.
In lofty shrouds the lookouts strain
  To pierce the white enclosing wall.

There is a prayer above in every mind,
  'Today!'
The dreary months in howling gale and spray
  All come to nought if we should miss
Again, to find
  The French have slipped away.

And so,
  When e'er we have the chance
We line the rails or ports and peer ahead
  And scan the misty unrevealing sky.
The sun, a faint and hazy distant light
  Still fails to drive the sea-mist
From our sight.
Upon the silent, softly heaving sea
  The fleet of Nelson, Collingwood
Line ahead,
  Urged by grim captains,
Pushing their bluff-nosed way,
  Sluggish, toward
The longed-for prey.

Breakfast!
  The order comes down the line,
We have the time
  But still the air is charged
With knowledge; beyond the mist
  Our destiny awaits.

The flanking frigates tack and
  Search as best they can;
The curtain thins; from where they lay concealed,
  'Mars', 'Thunderer', Colossus', 'Victory'
Are painfully revealed.

The morning marches, leaden. Still
   No sight, although we sense the sun
Get ever bright!
   We're ready, Aye
We're ready for the fight!

The minutes run down through
   The glass's, despairingly
The morning passes.

The lookouts in their circling tops
   Still peer
And hope; the sun draws high
   Until the whole horizon to the East
Is clear. And what a sight!
   What sight to greet the eye.
Their line of ships
   Appears to fill the sky!
We stare and gape
   Full straight ahead the enemy
Across Trafalgar's cape.

We roar and stamp and sing and shout;
   We open ports and see the guns run out.
The French meanwhile 'up helm' and
   Put about!
Elated now we close, two columns
   Side-by-side advance, each line ahead.

Racing, cursing all delay
   We've heard our captains say,
'We're going to break their column
   With our lines and do it Nelson's way.'

Now close upon their fleet, brave with signals
   'Victory'

Has almost reached their line, then Collingwood,
   In 'Royal Sovereign' and we
Not far behind.
   A puff of smoke, a splash ahead
Shot from a Spanish gun.
   'Three cheers for Nelson and the king',
The battle has begun'.

THE VASE
(1972)

The vase is unlike other jugs
   With handle or a spout,
It's made to put and store things in
   And not for pouring out.
Sometimes they can be found in pairs
   Like braces or like shoes;
They come in different colours,
   Green, orange or mixed hues.
You'd hear a vase collector sing
   With joy to get a jar from Ming.

The ancient Greeks had vases
   Made of earthenware they fired.
They painted scenes or patterns on
   By artists who perspired
And sweated in the hot Greek sun
   To get their scenes completed.
They did them standing up on racks
   Or else they did them seated.

I had a vase, a dirty thing
   All covered up with dust.

>I cleaned it up one early spring
>   And cleaned off all the rust.
>I chipped out all the cobwebs
>   And crushed up all the dirt;
>I dropped the chisel on my foot
>   And muckied-up my shirt.
>And after all the things I did
>   It only fetched me half-a-quid!

THE OLD GODS
(1969)

Unstirring, frozen in the depths of time
    The Old Gods sleep
Lost amidst the ancient hills.
    And all around the world
Continues on its headstrong way.
    The milling, teeming, thronging mass
Uncaring of the day.
    The minutes, hours, dash gaily on,
Take heed, care what I say.
    For when you stop to look about
And find your span of time run out.

Time's been and gone, wasted,
    Squandered and spent.
The fruitless search, born of envy,
    Spurred on by the jealous eye
Which sees with greed.
    But the dark worm of fear, mistrustful
Gnaws insidious,
    Distorting beauty,
Lauding hideous.
    And still the Old Gods sleep

Within the hills, sublime and deep.

He sleeps, old greybeard,
    Locked within his family
In centuries of sleep.
    Uncaring and untroubled
Unlike I, who
    Fearful of the future
Stand and sigh.

WATCHER ON THE SHORE

Standing lonely on the softly blowing sand
    As the sea retreats glistening from
The shore,
    With the texture as of silk within
His hand
    And the knowledge that the world's
Forever more,
He closes his eyes with face
    Uplifted to the wind,
Bathing in the golden beams of
    Evening sun
In that unity with Earth since Adam sinned,
    With contentment that
The day's full course is run.

Whilst the sun descends from out
The brazen sky
    And gleaming sea rolls onward to
The shore in heaving waves that soak away and
    Softly die,
The mystic turns into the night –
    Is seen no more.

NEMESIS (1)

And then he saw the misty hand of fate
    And felt the icy chill of its presence
As it approached.
    It gently pressed upon his chest
And rested there, lightly.

Its icy penetration struck his heart
    And brought panic-stricken numbness
To his whirling brain.
    'It is today,' it seemed to say
While resting there, lightly.

'You've freely run, unhindered by restraint
    But now your soul is
Marked and numbered.'
    Then, t'was gone!
His body lies with staring eyes
    And looks so – unsightly.

NEMESIS (2)

He saw the cold hand of Fate
    And felt the icy chill if its presence
As it approached.
    It gently pressed upon the softness
Of his chest
    And rested there – lightly.

The chill from it's fingers bored
    In deep penetration to his heart
And seemed to say,
    'You have run freely without restraint

But now
> Take heed – I have you marked.'

THERE IS SILENCE IN THE LANDSCAPE OF TOMORROW'S MEMORY

No-one will say, for shame
Why today can't forever be,
Like I do when I smile at my own
Burgeoning spring.
Streets full of shouts
And shopkeepers who sing,
And our own brand of
Boisterous, swaggering men,
Whom we saw now-and-then.
Not like the scruffy drunks of today
Who clear the streets of children,
Denying play
With their thuggery, buggery mayhem!
But nostalgia persists
In rainbow technicoloured
Sweet scented life;
The wholesome sweat of man,
Child and wife.
The smell of remembered home.

FACTORY FLOWERED UTOPIA

They have taken my mem'ries
And cast them aside
As aimless I linger in angular glass that repels.
For tomorrow's nostalgia I search

      For a seed
           But in barren Utopia there's
      Nothing to feed
           The mem'ries
                 And senses
      I once knew so well.
           Only desolate Bayberry,
      And how sharp the smell
           Of
      That infertile, damned
      Inanimate Factory Flower.

I WANT TO GO BACK...

I want to go back to my life again
And forget that ever I heard of his name
      And regain
    The world that I knew.
A world as familiar and personal to me
  As the sky up above me is blue.

For the sky is the same all over the world
     To bathers and sleepers
     There on their bed curled
      It's still the same sky
        Overhead.

Only, none of the sky looks the same.
So why should the rest of my life take the blame?
    For passively being consumers
        And users
Of false-promised things that are always the same?

WHITE OUT

Here is the night,
   The fading light
And darkness overwhelms.
   The secret shadows lengthen;
Unseen,
   The beginning of the nightmare dream
Beneath the wind
   As the world closes in
Within
   The limit of sight
In
   The night.

Close your eyes;
   Sleep care away
Until the coming of the day.
   All is well,
Fear dispel,
   For we can see
As far, as far, as far, as far may be.

Only –
   I would say, Fear not the night
For in the night is light.
   And though in daylight bright
You may see all the world
   'Tis only in the night
You see Eternity unfurled.

As far as eye can see
   The brightness of the stars gleams
Against the dark Eternity.
   Do you really know

What it means?
   Go to the furthest star and look beyond;
There, a different zodiac
   Set in a new Heaven.
And at that limit
   Look again, and see
A pattern of new worlds
   Again, again, again...
 For always and forever is it so.
   Never repeating
Always receding, beyond
   The limits of imagination.
Now suppose that you could see
   Everything revealed
Unto eternity.
   The overlapping pinpricks of the stars
That blend and merge until
   - no single star- but all Creation
Astonishing and bright.
   For instead of Earthly darkness
The night sky would be white!

THE MUSIC OF THE SPHERES

I am poised,
   Standing on the brink of
An ocean without sound.
   I am poised,
To hear the silence and serenity
   I've found.
I close my eyes
   And open up a Universe instead,
A kaleidoscope of galaxies it seems
   Within my head.

And I can fly,
  And I can die
To live forever
  For my life no longer counts
Its span in years.
  And I exist in perfect harmony,
Adrift upon the constant wave of music,
  The music of the spheres.

I can see
  A world within a world
In perfect harmony.
  Only me
Upon the limit of
  The dark Eternity.
But in the night
  The voice within
Said, 'Be there light.'
  And there appeared before my eyes
Beyond the limit of the skies
  The incandescent,
Omnipresent,
  From life preceding
To death receding
  A Universe eternal and
The banishment of fears.
  And as we drift upon this Earth
We trust the Star that gave us birth
  To be
In perfect harmony with
  The music of the spheres.

AN ELEGY
(After Southey)

Beneath the dishrag greyness of the sky
    Life, drained of colour dawdles
On its way.
    No sun to brighten Heaven up on high,
Light filters down and
    Paints the landscape grey.
The squirrel scampers, desp'rate in the wood
    And valiant snowdrops try to
Herald spring,
    All's waiting, save the river in its flood,
For life's renewal, that warmth and
    Sunshine bring.
The short days lengthen, inch by inch it
    Seems; forgotten pleasures
Rise in mem'ries dreams.
    We long to pass from winter's
Dismal chill
    And stroll in sunshine through
A dappled glade. Well here's a hope,
    A pleasure from Seville,
Hurrah for Richard and his marmalade.

WANDERJAHRE

The journeyman Years

THE LOVER

THE LOVER

When I shall die
Think only this of me;
There is some corner
In a tender heart
That is forever Brian

When I return
In mem'rys fading hue,
Remember in some gentle,
Fleeting phrase
The love I shared with you.

MY SOUL'S HAVEN

I have my heart,
I have my soul
But it takes you to make me whole.
Oh what would I, and what could I
Have been if left alone?
A lesser man
Without you here to care for me
Safe within our home.

IN THE WAKE OF SIEGFRIED

Gone! – am I gone?
Believe me, whilst ever you remember,
A part of me remains
In the music of our shared delights.

Listen, stay with me and remember
As I drift out upon the darkness,
Receding unseen into my dark eternal night
I will leave a tiny echo,
Unheard except in the stillness of your dreams,
The essence of my love,
To my love,
My best and truest friend.

THE GHOST

I have been the hero of my own life
  For I have fought with
The Dragons of Despair, and communed
  With the Angels of Euphoria.
I live, it seems, within my mind
  In mem'ries that rise from shadows
Like a sun-dispelling mist; the diffuse light
  Alternate bright and fleeting,
Sharp flickering then receding, tantalising,
  Leaving – no substance.
Until a sound forgot, a scent, faint whisper
  Of a sense more powerful, more intense,
A needle-point from brain to heart;
  And life's fleeting memories
Begin anew.
  For there are ghosts that walk.

I see them, beaming, happy
  In the pre-selected substance of
My dreams.
  The unlooked-for elegance of a bridge.
The whirring beat of wings, insistent power
  Slipping by,
Swans stroking, surging in slow measure,
  Thrusting along a still water to
The time worn, care-and-commerce worn
  Chipped and rope-harness worn
Serenity of red brick, a bridge made for
  The landscape,
An artefact to make sweet nature complete.
  Drips – timeless drips – echo small,
Ringing small in sullen water shaded in the
  Echo of its wall until time is broken
In the busyness of trade.
  Clip-clop, tick-tock
A barge, deep loaded to the cill
  Slips by
Stirring rushes, moorhens
  Water-rats and voles,
Ignored with indifferent disdain
  By the gently bobbing swans in
The gentle wake of iron-shod horses.
  And in quiet streets beyond,
The ring of voices, chiming in friendship,
  Warmed by love live on.

I am the ghost.
  For their time is not Past
When the future can look back and see
  Their Present.
And so I turn and whirl and turn again
  Within my time at a sound,

A childish trumpet sound, clear,
   Sentimental in the air, 'Oh Mein Papa'
And he is there.
   And Oh, how I yearn for the soft
Elusive touch.
   But paternal love could not be,
Not then, not even now. And beneath
   The weight of his world
His shadow falls about me, and holds me
   In an unrepentant dream.
Not with love at all
   But only as a supplicant, held in thrall.
He cannot change his future,
   I cannot change the past,
Or soften discontent,
   Or assuage
Rage,
   Or break the carapace of isolated grief,
Or plumb the depth of pity
   He rejected.
Move on, I cannot intercede.
   Nor could I then
When his suffering made my boyish love
   Recede.
For there is another shadow,
   Darker than mine, locked
In the solitude of madness.
   Move on!
There is no pain in memory
   Nor can a ghost feel, only watch
As a child watches until… until…
   For God's sake move on!
To the gentle watered landscape.

They are looking for me, I know.
   But I have taken his rejection

And made it my own.
   Now I reject them in my turn
With Oh! – such regret.
   And they cannot know how often
I stand at their side in my past,
   A ghost, returning from
The shadows of the future
   They gave with Love
To me.

HOW CAN I SAY…?

How can I say how lucky I've been
   To have joy and the love of you?
Always, always you have been there
   To love,
            To care.
Does need produce the hour?
   You will never know
How I needed you so
   When you filled that need
And nursed my secret, aching heart.

How I wish that I too
   Could leave something for you,
Something of pleasure and beauty
   For the world
To look upon with amazement and awe,
   And whisper together as you
Pass among them,
   'What a woman she must have been
To raise a man to such power, to nourish
   Such a seed upon such stony ground.'

TWO LIVES

I have lived two lives,
    Two lives in my life.
One was the life of my mind
    Filled with colour and light
And with love and delight
    Where Creation existed, unbound.
For the Universe doesn't exist beyond stars
    In man's external failure to see;
The Universe lives in a morsel of life,
    The Universe lives within me.

I have lived two lives,
    Two lives in my life.
One was a life of denial, subjecting my will
    To the will of another,
Condemned to a self-imposed trial.
    To deny my own intellect
To that of a fool, to deny truth for ignorance
    I am the tool and squandered my time.
Oh such ignorant folly
    To deny my Divinity.
That is my crime.

TO MY 'JUDY-LOO'
(1986)

Above all, we have each other.
    Has it really been so many years?
Why, in my heart I feel like 25 again
    With all to work for with ambition's
Fiery flame. But not, perhaps,
    So filled with rage

As when you first knew me, and blind
    Impotence made me
Despair and fight against the limits of
    My world.

And you, my love, my 'Judy-Loo'
    What would I be if not for you?
The days run headlong into one,
    A blur of distant memory.
Only you and I are constant.

Was it all a preparation for this,
    The recurring pleasure of your kiss?
Two young people sharing
    The pleasures of this passing life,
Two spirits wand'ring hand-in-hand
    Across the world?

I live within the eddies,
    The miracle of music.
Hear me and take my hand again
    As I fall like long-remembered melody,
Note-by-note upon your ears.
    Hark, and catch the soft and gentle tears
Within the sight and sound of
    Sunlight and the wind,
And clouds of passing rain,
    And listen – and hear it once again,
The essence of my enraptured heart
    Beating,
Fleeting and elusive
    Within that last refrain.

HOME IS WHERE THE HEART IS

Home is where the heart is
And my heart is in the West
In a city by a river where
The white swan builds her nest
And the green cathedral cloister
Offers refuge from the heat
And the hustle
And the bustle
Of the busy city street.
And I loiter there and listen
With my senses all replete,
And re-capture childhood's magic
From that shady cloister seat.
Rememb'ring my first family
(the ones I loved the best)
Who provided that rare childhood
In that city in the West.

ALL THE WORLD I HAVE

All the world I have,
And all the joy and pleasure that I see,
The tripping, laughing sun lit days,
So many days (the ones you gave to me)
My endless life.

I look ahead to years,
Happy, fruitful contented years;
The warmth of your smile upon me,
Your hand held in mine.

I have a world within my head.
It is a boundless world of flower scents
And deep mysteries,
Of faerie woods
And the great majestic spirit
Weaving through the starry Universe.
And the kaleidoscope world,
Brilliant and moody;
The great enthralling music of
My World.

My life. My life is a rich cascade
Of love and happiness.
I have no gold, only this,
My world.
And now I find it hard to say, can say no more
Save,
'My world, I lay this world, this treasure
At your door.'

ON JUDY'S BIRTHDAY

Birthdays are to give you memories
Of sunlit squares and shady passages,
And destinations filled with happiness,
Languid, lapping sea and beaches
Keep life's pleasures
In our reaches.

Happy day my Dearest Jude,
A crowning day of year,
Your Anniversary,
A ribbon of anniversaries

From childhood parties to today's,
All along the years.
Happy Birthday my Dear Jude.
Add this to the ribbon of your memories.
Oh Happy Day.

ON SIXTY-NINE
(2010)

How many years I've known you?
How many years together?
None of the hours and minutes matter
As long as you are there.

How many smiles in my memory,
Shining through your eyes?
How many times can I tell you I love you?
A million times are but once,
Scattered along our lives.

But 'I love you' – again.

TO JUDY
(2007)

….and love is blind,
Sees nothing through the eyes
But through the mind.
And love is weak,
For broken hearts can only bleed
When false love is unkind,
And turn the other cheek.
And love is me,

For if I couldn't see
But had to know you just by touch,
Why then, I'd love you just as much,
And take your hand, your hand sublime
(It means so much,
Our fingers inter-twined).
And hearts,
Two hearts
That beat as one,
And hope as one
And never, never parts.

MY LIFELONG LOVE
(1991)

In half a century of living
  I have lived a range of lives,
Through boyhood, adolescence, youth
  Been reckless, never profound, wise.
But manhood must be counted best
  Which puts all learning past
Unto the test.
  For throughout all I have been blessed
With love and comfort, spirits rest
  By you – my love – my lifelong love,
From first to last the Best of Wives
  Who helped me live
My range of lives.

A HEAVEN

Let us make it then
   A heaven of
Our own, a place of
   Comfort, happiness and love.
Our home, a universe,
   A world within the world
For us.

THE GARDEN OF MY LIFE

In the garden of my life
  Are many, many days of rainbow light
Which sparkle through the rain. Freshed in
  Drips and droplets following the storm.
And rising warm above the thrusting blooms
  And spring-green shoots of newborn
Inspiration,
  Your love. The sunshine in my soul.

I feel like fertile earth, while shooting
  Thoughts give birth to weed and tack,
The choking undergrowth of my mind.
  But still the flowers grow,
The sweet smell of Rose and Honeysuckle
  Above all.

In the garden of my life where mossed and
  Broken paving wends its crazy way,
There is, despite all, symmetry and pattern;
  Where flowers of bright experience
Stand high beyond steady lawns.
  And, freesia-sweet, love's perfume

Mingles in the heady air. And over all
   Is calm and peace
When I've your love to share.

A DECLARATION

O wife thy husband loves thee, forever
   At your call.
He'll kiss, caress and care for you;
   Lay all his secrets bare for you,
But most of all be there for you.
   So have no fear, he's always near
To give for you his all.

O son thy father loves thee with
   Tenderness and pride.
With happiness he'll reach to you,
   Fair play he'll try to teach to you
- Be honest – he'll beseech to you.
   And when you ever need a friend
You'll find him by your side.

O daughter small and helpless, contented
   Be your sleep.
Your brother loves and cares for you,
   And mother's always there for you
With love, each day to share for you.
   So little one dream safely on,
My watch o'er you I'll keep.

My family I love you, although it may
   Not show
When deep frustrations make me mad

Your disappointment, bleak and sad
Brings home to me the things we had;
　Contentment, happiness and love,
These things to you I owe.

A RECANTATION
(1980)

Long evenings stretching into night
　We talked.
Do you recall how, long and mellow,
　As the shadows matched our mood
We explored our joint belief
　(Leavened with some light relief)
Whilst the golden sunset blue'd
　And long,
Long, summer evenings stretched
　Into the night?
We perceived with joy each other
　Sharing Universal truths, pushing
The bounds of inspiration, seeking
　To pierce the veil of mystic ignorance.

So close we felt;
　One more step, a reach of insight
And we should pluck the forbidden
　Fruit of knowledge
From the bough.
　A sense of it was almost there
And there is so little
　That we really know.

But now I ask, 'Why seek?'
　Rather would I turn my back

On the unresolved forever.
   For we stand upon a threshold
From wherein
   Temptation says,
'Come, and I will bring you Revelation.
   And who, faltering, enters,
Leaves behind their empty, earthbound shell.'
   Rather would I spend a thousand years
With you in blissful ignorance…

ROOM 207 – GARDA YOUR SECRETS

Garda your secrets like the depth
Of the placid lake where, alone
I swim within you,
Enfolded in your sublime depths, your
Deep, exhausting sublime depths,
Your heart, soul and body entwined
And flowing over mine...
Garda your secrets.

A DISTILLATION OF MEMORY

The days of my life
Are shrouded in time
And the sweet joys of manhood
Enjoyed in my prime
Are fleetingly precious to me.
The joy of your happiness shows in your smile
As you linger, content, in my arms
For a while
As the mist of my mem'rys distilled.

So here's to the secret life
Of Love and sheer delight,
Of pleasure granted from above
The fever of the night.
Oblivious to other care
This life of Loving that we share.
Oh darling wanton – oh, my wife –
How tenderly you come to me
Then reckless, breathless passion soon
To end with love's requited swoon.

The mem'ries are alive today,
The way we were and still remain.
Tho' years may pass no minutes lost
When Love is given reckless reign
To sweet oblivion in your arms,
And tenderness, desire insane
We think we'll never see again.
I see it still within your eyes
The Love, the lust shorn of disguise.

And seeing you and seeing me
In youth the way we used to be
My mind recalls my senses reeling,
More than mem'ry, life's real feeling.
The tender softness of your skin,
Your eyes invite me to begin.

Oh sweet joys of manhood
So precious and so rare
Can never, ever really fade
While you lay with me there.

JUDITH BY ANOTHER NAME

Hark! – the silent music of the Queen,
        The unknown, unseen Queen,
My Mab – Mab of the faeries,
        Mab, Queen of all Delight
Who comes, triumphant
        Quiet and serene,
Mistress of the dark
        Dew-dappled night.

Against the misty window,
        In unspoken words
That urge to pleasure, matching
        Sighs in measure;
Flitting, glimmering,
        Fragrant, shimmering
The Faerie moon pervades the room
        And all is lost in sublimating rapture,
Woven and captured in Mab's smile…

A world beyond the world
        The Moonglow
Bathing all, and worldly things
        Transgress;
Eternity beckons, briefly
        'till all is lost again.
Just the dappled moon, the faerie room
        In soft, receding eternity of time.
Only Mab, my Queen of Queens,
        Consuming passion of
All my earthly dreams
        Remains, close in my arms.

ON FINDING THE IMPRINT OF JUDY'S LIPSTICK ON A TISSUE

These are the lips,
 The tender lips,
The lovely lips I kissed.
 They do not fade
Or turn from me
 But always softly yield
To love and passion,
 Tenderness, and all
Of love's delight.
 As long as lips like these
Touch mine
 The world is mine tonight.

I THINK OF YOU
(1982)

I think of you in Scotland,
 I think of you in Slough.
Oh how I wish you were with me
 And I was with you now.

I miss the way you look at me,
 The softness of your touch.
Whenever we are parted Ju
 I miss you oh! – so much.

A VALENTINE FOR 69
(2010)

I believe there are faces hidden in the sky.
  I believe, and hear their voices
Woven in the breeze.
  All those I loved are blended
In the landscape of the trees.
  And I believe the love we share
Between us, no less than
  That of Dante or of Venus
Is a wonderful, divine, sublime
  Creative thing that
Frees the soul, and sets it on a wing.
  And when I think of you, a feeling
So intense
  Arises from within, a Seventh Sense
That sets my soul alight
  And makes
My heart to sing.

My song will never cease,
  Nor will my heart decay
For love is immemorial
  And lives from day-to-day.
Refreshed, inspired in mem'ries
  Of all we've been.
For true love – my love –
  Mysterious, unseen
My love for you
  Can never fade away.

These then are the voices,
  The sounds that call to me.
The images of those who loved
  Smile 'love' from eternity.

Yours is the heart that beats,
  And beats within the heart of me.
For this I know,
  All that I am,
Far greater than the whole
  You – yes 'you' reside within me,
You – my very heart,
  My soul.

THE NUTCRACKER, MY SWEET

Where sunshine fills the golden room by day
  And when the moon by night
Shines silver light
  And stars come out to play,
And meadows stretch to
  Distant hills
And all the view with gladness
  Fills
Your heart,
  Then I will love you.

WENN TROMPETEN SPIELEN…

I heard a trumpet trio sound
  Three notes, and Angel voices called;
My soul leaped up to be unbound
  And in my sleep I was enthralled,
For in my slumber I was blessed
  And called to my Eternal rest.
It was the end of Earthly day,
  And so I left and slipped away,

My journey through my life complete.
   I see your tears, I see you weep
But know from me, that Love survives
   And spreads beyond our Earthly lives.
For we have loved as lovers should,
   And so across the void on high
Though Angels weep to see you cry
   Your tears are seen and understood.

Remember then with tender smiles;
   Remember for our precious years
For all around I am with you,
   I'll bring you comfort, calm your fears.
And I will wait and I'll be true
   Until the trumpet calls and you
Will join with me to be re-bound
   By Angels, when their trumpets sound.

THE CYNIC

AGENT ORANGE – VIETNAM
(A defoliant whose side-effect is children with Hydrocephalus)

It is not a joke so please don't laugh
   But after years of fine research
In hospital and patho' lab
   (and still not knowing what's the cure)
We now can make more Hydrocaphs.

And when you want to go and kill
   You say you have the right,

And spend enormous treasure
  To support your need to fight.

But when its over and you leave,
  Retreating up the path
You say, 'Its not our problem now,
  (we have no right, it's not our fight)
And don't provide a little change
  To help our Hydrocaph.

LIFE WAS BRIGHT

Can you believe that life was bright
  And sweet within a cattle truck?
Amongst the filth and muck?
  In the gloom, locked out of sight?
(No light,
  No room) just pressed
And herded all upon each other,
  Father, child, wife and mother...
I saw it all but now
  I can't recall
Each passing scene
  Is just a dream, retaining nothing
Save even at this extreme
  'Life is sweet.'

I think it's time that hurts the most. It's there,
  No sooner there, than gone,
No sooner looked upon my wife, my son
  Than a century is passed within
The twinkling of an eye.
  You dare not pray
Nor even pay

Attention even to
The splendid beauty of
  A songbird calling in the wood,
For then that precious moment too,
  Squandered in delight,
Like all the world is gone.

LET ME COUNT THE FIRST THOUSAND
(Berlin, Dresden, Liverpool, Sheffield, London, Nagasaki et al)

Let me count the first thousand
  Who hurry and run;
Let me number their fears
  For their own minds are dumb
And the souls of the just
  Echo in silence,
In pools of indifference,
  Cocooned in the sound
That drives away pity,
  In silent screams drowned…

Let me count the first thousand;
  Each made up of one
Out of time, out of life,
  Out of hope, out of fear;
Running and stumbling
  As horror draws near
In the wailing from heaven
  That shatters the brain
Of those who remain
  In their sorrow and pain
In the hope they're the last
  Of the dead who remain.

Let me count the first thousand,
  The victims we saw
Who begged and entreated
  The end of all war.
But across the horizon
  Unseen, yet to come
Hear the dreadful, familiar beat of the drum,
  And the numbers are legion
And the legions are dumb;
  Let me count the first thousand
For look, here they come...

THE GREAT PRETENDER

The man in the suit
  Didn't know how to shoot
He was far too astute
  And too selfish, to boot.
But he still took the praise
  (It was like this always).

The man in the suit
  Pushed himself to the fore
And he puffed and he preened,
  Said, 'I've just fought a war.'
And he lies, and denies
  There was no cause for strife.
But the cost of his lies
  Was another man's life.

TO THE TOWN-HALL PRINCES
(1998)

Don't tell me that you won't,
   Don't tell me that you wouldn't!
Don't tell me that you didn't,
   Don't tell me that you couldn't;
Don't tell me that you're English
   And because of that you can't,
For I've seen the lie
   Gleam in your eye
Despite the spoken word
   Uttered with supreme aplomb,
Don't tell me I'm absurd!
   It's easy when 'procedure'
Can dictate what you say,
   Things like, 'Frankly sir
We do not care
   So kindly go away.'
Then return to your contented life
   In the knowledge that the needy
And the undeceiving poor
   Have been shown to
Their accustomed place
   And ushered to the door!
So don't tell me you wouldn't
   'Cos I know that you did.
D'you know what I'm referring to?
   D'you think I'm just a kid?
It's your cold, self-righteous duty
   Without question or a qualm,
Impervious to the harm
   You perpetrate.
How carelessly
   You promulgate
Unrest and hate!

THE MOUNTEBANKS
(1964)

In lavish robes stand serried ranks
   Of varied pompous mountebanks,
Pontif-icating, looking down
   With sneering supercilious frown,
Declaiming in their piety upon
   Upon the sin of Man.
But their hypocrisy is worse
   Than those who Dogma criticise,
But understand the Fear of God
   But cannot tolerate the rantings
And all the avaricious pantings
   Of Church.
The 'princes' who profess to be
   The very glass of charity,
Whose pomp and majesty proclaim
   Their rise in rank in Jesu's name.
But they are shown
   Upon their throne
As dog who snatches juicy bone;
   Who say, 'We're good men,
One and all.'
   But if you were to stumble,
Fall from what they say are Christian ways
   Then see their – perhaps –
Mocking gaze.
   What place have gilded robes and hats
When people starve or else eat rats?
   Think now and ponder at your leisure
Why Christian church should
   Have such treasure/
He taught, two thousand years ago
   That as ye reap, so shall ye sow;
Now reconcile this church's riches

With Him who taught in fields
And ditches.
So let them meet a dying nation's needs
And find their own salvation by their deeds.

MINE EYES HAVE SEEN TOO MUCH
(2009)

Mine eyes have seen too much
Of things such
As eyes aren't meant to see,
Or minds to feel.
Like joyful zeal
That sends a soul uplifted
With such high ideal,
Unthinking,
Eyes unblinking
In the sharp revealing light
Of expectation,
Into the night
Just like before
And will do
Forevermore.
It can't be right
To send our youth
With arguments of false
Corrupted truth
Into the blight
Of bloody war.
For I have seen beyond
The false-promised glory,
And watched the sombre
Lining of the village street

> Turned out to greet
> The victims of betrayal.
> Mine eyes have seen too much.

I KNOW WHAT I KNOW – I THINK
(The Rumsfeldt Doctrine)

> I know what I know;
>> What I don't know
> I don't.
>> And there's the things
> That we don't know,
>> We do.
> And the sly mind that says
>> There are things that we knew
> Are the things that we don't know
>> That really are true.
> For there's still things we don't know
>> We don't know at all.
> Oh the logic of minds
>> That hold us in thrall,
> That deceive us and blind us
>> And blinds itself too.
> It's a criminal fool
>> Who believes
> He deceives
>> Me and you.
> But - we let him,
>> We do.

> And we all acquiesce
>> As we're trying to guess
> And try to divine

        Just what he'll say next,
What's behind
        The mad text
That, driven by greed
        Is meant to mislead!
And though we may scoff
        In impotent fury
At liars who lie
        It's the mothers who cry;
It's our children who die.

HOW MANY BLED...?

How many bled that one July
  Beneath a sky that promised else
A summer day of peace?
  A picnic, boating on the Wye,
Other tranquilities that seemed
  Nevermore to cease.
Only a brief remembrance,
  With beating heart –
Not hearts of love, not now,
  Not this vile day –
The only hearts that beat with love
  Are far away, not these
Hoping for a hero's pride,
  The swagger of a safe return,
A forlorn clinging to
  Sternly held belief.
Refusal to be hoodwinked
  By the grim deception in
The telegram received,
    'An honourable death.'

Rows of carved memorials
　Line the path
Beneath the trees.
　Were you really glad he went?
Or are you haunted still
　By memories of him
And other men?

THE FATE OF MAN

It was a pearl, a pearl of lustrous blue,
　A clear translucent, vibrant,
Perfect hue.
　Set in the dark it glowed with life
'Till something dark within
　Upon it grew.
Clouds of microbe life which knew
　That covering the pearl
Would smother it!
　But reckless of that knowledge
It ate its way and etched into the pearl
　Until the lustrous light of life
Was dimmed.
　And when the microbes saw, and tried
To restore the bloom of life and
　　Redeem the fateful blunder, too late,
The pearl they had ransacked for plunder
　Was dead,
Smothered in the microbe host instead.

REFLECTIONS ON A LOST CAREER

I came to you a hero,
Welcomed with a cheer,
The saviour of the company,
'We're glad to have you here.'
But now I view you
With contempt
And me – I hear you sneer –
What has he done?
He's useless
He'll be out within the year...

HOME THOUGHTS FROM ACROSS THE GREAT DIVIDE

You stand and weep and say I'm 'glorious'
  Now that I'm no longer there,
But I remember now when you
  Abused me on the square.
'Have some fun with new-found friends',
  'Learn a trade and become skilled',
But ne'er a word behind the 'fun',
  Never a word that I'd be killed.
The foe, it was said, we'd defeat
  'Over there'
But the real torment came
  In the garrison square,
Where ideals are scattered
  And dreams count for nought,
Where lives count for nothing
  In political sport.

So now your only comfort
   As unseen I hover by
Is to stand with sombre feelings,
   While a tear wells in your eye,
With the great and good
   Who pledged their honour
Well I did not pledge mine,
   I gave you more
I gave my life,
   I gave my unspent time!
But standing stern and upright,
   Rigid with regret,
They ask more men to follow me –
   It isn't over yet!
And they'll be used
   Because they're young
And follow with
   Life's song unsung,
Silenced to the whim of fools,
   Their prejudices and their rules
That make no sense nor have no reason,
   Relics of another season
Where the sacrifice of others
   Distributes more grief to mothers.

THE IDEALIST

A GOOD DAY'S LIFE

Talking and working, walking and shirking
Humming and running, happiness drumming,
   Making progress to where?
   Do we care?

Well I do.
It's not so much for rich reward
(Why do I dwell upon that theme?)
But happiness and recognition,
'What you do is good,'
No – more than that –
Better than you'd hoped.
For fame itself's
Not good enough
Self-satisfaction is the thing.
You may deceive the others
But you can't deceive yourself.

THE HERD – A TERMINAL EXPERIENCE

There is blankness in the eye
Of those who, helpless sigh
In an endless waiting throng;
Who while shuffling along
Are mindless, numb,
Staring, dumb.
What lies ahead?
Such fear, such dread
While others, new arrived
Join the shuffling passers by
Casting similar bemused eyes;
What time? Which way?
Confined today
Then exhortation, angst deflected
By brisk imperative directed,
Vulnerable and unprotected
From vague fears; a sudden rush
Out of life
Within the milling, aimless strife.

They're all the same,
The fearful fidgets, anxious strain
Until – relieved –
They're safely on the 'plane.

RIDING THE WIND

Riding, eyes glazed, ecstatic
Upon a rush of wind,
Exalted high into the heavens,
Riding the sky;
With tendril arms that weave
And seek with searching
Sensing fingers for
The magic pulse of Life.
Adrift. Alone and falling
Through the kaleidoscope
Of multi-coloured sky,
Hair streaming, chiffon streaming,
Plummet gaily in
Reckless abandon to the Earth.
Now with growing fear
As hard and rocky ground grows near,
Down through howling wind
And cloud.
Trees, rising trees,
Tears, red-rimmed streaming eyes
In headlong plunge.
It's here, oh pray
A second more,
Now, now!
And blankly astonished
A smile, relief profound

Float downward to the ground
And land, slightly shocked but otherwise
Unharmed
As light as thistledown.

MINSTREL BOY

Minstrel boy, minstrel boy
  Bring me your music,
Take up your lute or guitar
  In your hand.
You have a talent and now
  You should use it
And sing your lament for the loss of
  This land.
So play your song softly and make
  Your voice sad,
And sing of the comfort and grace
  That we had.

Minstrel boy, minstrel boy sing of
  Our childhood,
For laughter and innocence crowding
  Each day,
When legends and heroes filled all
  Our horizons
And spiced our imagined adventures
  At play.
So gently and softly now, play me
  Your song
And cherish the mem'ry of childhood
  That's gone.

Minstrel boy, minstrel boy

Sing me to slumber
And dreaming I'll capture the
Freedom of youth;
Of leaping and running, competing
And winning
And daring and facing each
Moment of truth.
So play for young heroes
With vigour and grace
Who uncertain, unknowing
Their futures must face.

A MIDSUMMER NIGHT'S...

Long and gentle is the soft-drawn sigh
Of darkness over the lawn
Where dandelion clocks tick noiseless,
For night, unfolding dusky wings
Has banished light
And daylight things
To memory
Of sunset flaring glorious amongst
High castle-clouds,
And swallows, wheeling, chase
Elusive insect flies
Until
All is still.
Trees murmur in shadows
And you are abandoned to the dark
And...
Sleep. Sleep, soft and warm,
Drowsing in the heat of
Summer night, cool hand beneath
The pillow and the secret, inner eye

Opens to His dark, fearsome world.

Here in a cot, gently rocking, sleeping,
   Slumb'ring beneath
The faerie pattern woven in the sheet.
   Reach out, draw back, dare you see
The baleful lurking monster? No.
   Turn instead in fear, moving
Along dark rows where cherubs sleep
   Until – turn the coverlet!
Swarthy with bristle the glittering
   New-born infant eye turns upward
Toward night, fearful.
   Above the sheet dawn stands
Grey against the curtain and blessed relief
   Rises like the warmth of blankets
As you turn and sleep, content again.

AN DIE MUSIK

Roam, high and free in spirit, adrift
Upon the sounds and waves of music.
Casting out, searching far beyond
The confines of mortal sense and sensibility;
Beyond our knowledge and understanding of
Chemical and Physical Law,
Aloft and free along waves and thought, Images conjured by
the inspiration of
The great musician;
Tchaikowsky, Beethoven, Brahms, Elgar
Releasing through their own inspired
Imaginings emotion, deep, physical
And with the magic of these, open
The greater Mind's images through

Which to roam.
If music is the key, then how soon
Is it lost when once
The mind is free?
And being free where then will it roam?
Amongst the great galaxy of stars,
Sensing the isolation and freedom which
It brings?
The solitude and
Spirit-cleansing chill?
Ah yes, the spirit,
This ephemeral
Something – magical
(Is that the word?)
Spark.
No! spark is too frail, thrusting upward
And away upon the smoky current.
Soul then; the soul, the very key of life,
Tough, intangible and being so, free
To roam within, without the confines of this
Universe.
Our home.

BACK TO THE AMAZON

I found myself today
  Back where I used to play.
On the forest banks of the mighty Amazon
  Whose shore is haunt of muddy
Crocodile, wary in the deep, and tangled
  Green serpents lurk and twine unseen,
And sun bursts over swirling water,
  Eddy and current, floating islands
Of entangled wood.

   Beware, beware the Indian
With poisoned dart.
   Cock your rifle, safari is
About to start.

Surprising how little change there's been.
   The rich black earth, the same
Tangled woods,
   The stream.
Except
   The maisonettes weren't there before,
In days of yore when,
   In childhoods high summer, my play
Took me to the Amazon,
   So far, so far away.

FOOLISH HASTE

Bittersweet you foolish, falling tear
I feel you sting my cloudy eyes again
For all that's lost.
Foolish, foolish
To count too soon the cost!

LIFE'S SAD REGRETS

What happened to the days
That life had promised me?
The mem'ries of 'Its good to be alive'?
Why is it that on waking,
For another life I'm aching
With the effort that I'm making
To face another day and to survive?
What happened to Integrity and Truth?
The virtues I was taught when in my youth?

Its time to do, not just to dream,
Though dreaming, as it does within the mind,
Allowing inspiration to unwind
Creates.
Yet now the dream is done.
Now – to make it fact –
Requires an act of will,
Some feat
To make the dream complete.
So here and there, and now and then
I take up pencil or a pen
And rush to verse
Or, what is worse,
Sit poised with furrowed brow
Lips pursed,
Thinking to unwind a theme
Or find an epic in a dream..

BEYOND THE VEIL

I dreamed that no-one knew me
In this strange, distant and familiar land.
Beneath the wild and massing clouds
That presaged evening time
I came along the track, wild
With broken flint and stone,
Cringing heather abounding brittle
On either side, receding dark
Across the moor.
And climbed with day-long weariness
Up, to the crest of the long,
Long slope.
And still no-one knew me,
Only eyes that followed.
And the long, wild wind skipping fresh
Across the crest
And I,
My coat drawn close
And my hair blown back
And nothing, still nothing,
No sound save the wind gushing strong
In my ears.

And a broken path that opened wide
Before a rough-hewn cottage
Broken, boarded door,
Crazy bolted shutters,
An old worn grinding stone set before,
And poverty, cold, harsh,
Shrouded in unremitting silence,
Denying its own need to me,
A helpless watcher,
Unseen, unknown,

Uncaring; grateful to wake
And shake
The dream away.

THE 'FEW'

In recent times above our homes
From motley scattered aerodromes,
Pretending they had not a care
They grimly fought, and died up there.

What waste of blood and fleeting fame
To deprecate as though ashamed
Their gift, the freedom granted many
With easy discontent and envy.

THE 'SHEAF'

I remember 'The Sheaf'
Where we ambled beneath
A mantle of brilliant stars.
In that night in that company
(Friendly and warm)
We were easy together and laughter was born,
And holidays planned with mem'ries of days
Crowned in the evening of sun's golden rays.
So we stroll to 'The Sheaf',
Its not far to go,
For a pint with our friends,
To meet Barrie and Jo.

TAKE ME TO THE MOUNTAINS

Take me to the mountains 'ere I die
   And lose me, deep in awe beneath the sky
In landscape all omnipotent
   Where dreams are born
And renewal comes to souls careworn
   By insignificance, the
Irritating whims, the meaning-less
   Pressing next half-hour,
The drudgery of shattered hopes,
   The misery of dreams gone sour.

Take me to thee, mountains, and I'll gaze
   In awe, seeking to re-capture the
Freedom that I felt before
   When all experience was new
And revelation matched my sense of wonder
   As senses reeled and set themselves
To plunder such magnificence
   And solitude within the world.
Oh, take me to the mountains.

THE PATRIOT'S GIFT

The aged patriot raised his fist
   And shook his cane with a feeble wrist
At the fervent, bright glazed eyes before,
   And spoke of glories won in war,
Invoking the spirit of Old Romance,
   And Chivalry armed with shield
And lance.

With fervent tears he implored,
'Advance! Lay down your lives and
Bleed for France!'

Oh, what a lowering was there then
Of the heart-rending valour
Of those young men,
Forsaking futures, sweethearts, wives
For a notion of 'glory;'
To lay down lives
For the gift that would immortalise
Their memory forever...

For the boys heard golden
Words of praise
And High Ideals transfixed their gaze
As Roads to Glory
Filled their minds
With misplaced pride,
Fanned by the love they left behind;
The tearful bride
Who yearned
As he turned
And left her side.
Forsaking all Love's tender charms
To march with brother men-at-arms,

.

In place of love-filled perfumed kiss
And scented breath
To find an end instead
In putrid, fly-blown death.

ENTROPY
(And God created the Universe, and it was perfect)

I know the journey I am on
   With you and they, those that
Have gone before, and others
   Yet to come;
A journey we have shared.
   It wasn't Eden long ago
Where man's great Odyssey began;
   The journey had begun long before
In deep Creation's stellar roar
   The Universe! -
An instant of perfection.
   But what if Cosmos were to die
And starlight vanish from the sky
   To give no pleasure to the eye?
Just blackest night and lifeless life,
   A residue of what we were,
A memory lost, and gone in flaring death
   Just like our Sun.
For life proceeds toward its Death
   As living man gives up his breath.
And secrets once revealed to see
   Would, from our understanding flee.
Will Heaven's journey, just like mine
   End in the blank demise of time?
No! For cosmos cannot be destroyed
   Just as it never was created,
But lives and swirls in formless void
   By will Divine
            In endless time…

Why strive to perfect Perfect Art?
   The certainty that knowledge brings
Is transient folly, like Fools Gold,

Exposing the conceit of kings.
For Perfect knowledge defies logic,
　　(who can divine the Divine will?)
Truth is the province of the poet;
　　The more we know, the less revealed.

So swirl, transmute and penetrate,
　　Explore and push at Heaven's gate
It will remain Perfection still
　　When mam's vain artefacts are gone.
And reaching backward into time
　　Will not reveal God's hidden Plan
And alchemy cannot reveal
　　What we can't know but only feel.
For God remains and His Creation
　　Moving, surging, swells unchanged.
(Unform it, it re-forms again;
　　See once more Creation's pain).
The ingenuity of Man
　　Can't comprehend what God began
And so, why seek to understand
　　The limits of an endless span,
Or time defined in timeless space?
　　Come, close your eyes,
Believe with me. You fear for
　　Universe destroyed?
Look – God's new Cosmos fills the void.

THE SHALLOW, FATUOUS FOOL
(Isherwood, my dear)

Safe with his circle, the
  Smile of fond recollection revealed
Perfection framing
  Unspoiled teeth
To listeners who hung at his feet
  Simpering, giggling
While he sipped life's Ambrosia.
  And told of his involvement,
A tourist of the war
  Recounting what he saw but
Not really 'seeing' – only
  The fascinating, shattered, frightened
Wretches who so entertained
  And became framed
In beautiful, light-hearted
  Words of unrepentant recollection
By this self-centre'd
  Liver of other people's lives,
Untouched by fellow-feeling.

And the listeners stared with eager
  Sycophantic giggles,
Their eager self-expression
  Giving bland encouragement,
A gleam, to his receptive eye, a
  Curl to the carefully disdaining lip
To the fellow-travellers of his indifference,
  Who revelled in the satisfaction of
His hideous self-assurance;
  Devoid, for all the gifts bestowed,
Of gratitude.
  Sans regard for fellow-man
Or others' feelings

In his detailed dealings
Of a self-indulgent, unblameworthy
Bland, sadistic vice.

Did I say 'fellow-feeling'?
What about the superficial flaunting
Of the vulgar to the uncomprehending
Misanthropic gaze?
Those sublime boys
(For such they then were) with
Scruples and ideals, descending
Through seductive depths of
Perverted intellect
To the corrupted, sunless waters
Of self-proclaimed, self-justified
Indulgence?
What of they?
That the sublime should be so vulgar!
That intellect should so deceive,
Concealing such brute ignorance!
That such smug self-justified attention
Should be so well perceived!

MYSTIC MIST
(An allegory)

There was mist upon the river
Life was stirring in the rushes
And cobwebs, heavy with the dew
Were hanging in the bushes.
And the moon was fading, waning
In the last deep shade of night
And silently, with no farewell

    Stars vanished out of sight
As the river softly shimmered,
   And the eddies
Gleamed and glimmered.
   And the world was waiting breathless,
Time was stilled and life was deathless.
   Like a miracle new day was born
As, slow and stealthy came the dawn.

But the paradise was fleeting
   In the land of peace and plenty,
For the bonds of trust were broken
   And the promises were empty,
For into the early morning light
   Wings of war soared into flight
And the singing of the skylark
   In the land of sweet content
Was replaced by soundless vapour trails;
   The peaceful sky was rent
By the wails of human sorrow,
   By the endless sad lament.
Dashed! – the promise of tomorrow,
   Dashed! – the joy of things to be,
Gone our hopes and waking dreams;
   God recedes
As mankind pleads.

Into the thoughts of waking day
   The consciousness of Sunlight streams.
The nightmare passes, dark thoughts wane
   And Hope prevails,
(Hope's not in in vain)
   The nightingale will sing again!
For Faith and Love dispel despair,
   With Truth and Knowledge
Tempered kindly

With the healing power of Prayer,
The Love that's true and Love sincere
The Love that loves and conquers Fear
Though mist conceals
True love's revealed.
For all the Earth beneath the skies
Approves with clear, untroubled eyes
When man and nature harmonise.

THE AGE OF ENLIGHTENMENT

Let's spread understanding
And wisdom around,
Let us not leave the Natural World
As its found,
But let us enlighten the primitive regions
Where innocence lives for
Their vices are legion.
So lets bring roads, communications,
Show them the United Nations,
Protocol, administrations,
Deadlines, plans and exploitation.
Lets replace their shells and bones
With Gold Cards, mobile telephones.
Let's show them how good it can be
When greed makes them like you and me,
With cars and roads,
And tanks and 'planes,
And sinks with overflowing drains.
So urbanise (forget what comes
With overcrowding in the slums).
Let's clear the jungle, let's build cities
And then declare, 'A thousand pities
For the poor, the squalid masses,'

Clinging to what barely passes
For a wholesome way of life
That's filled with war and
Thrives on strife.
Let's build and prosper on munitions,
Replace their tribes with politicians.
Let's…
No – let us please just go in peace
And show respect for simple tribes
And learn we mustn't touch their lives.
When avarice replaces need
The only thing we feed is greed.

THE SPACEMAN
(A cosmic paradox)

If I exist within a space
Then what conundrum now awaits
To reconcile space-time to this:
I am the Universe
Alone.

Within the Universal me
There stands another Adam's tree,
Another Eden not yet found,
Another Sun, another flame
As great a Cosmos, in my frame
As starry Universe above can claim.
A secret stored within my hand
As great as all the planets known,
That's greater then the mind can span,
For in the Cosmic Paradox
I am a sub-atomic man.

I am mere space, my scale unfixed,
  A cosmos, swirling galaxies,
Each molecule an atom's child,
  A nucleus, electron cloud,
A perfect structure, undefiled;
  Mirroring known fact and form,
Decays when dead and grows when born.

Each Cosmic echo of Creation
  (Crude measurement of light or time)
Man looks in vain for 'infinite'
  Confined within the narrow mind.
I carry Cosmos in the texture
  Of my skin, my hair, my bone,
So here's Creation's paradox
  (What is the scale you comprehend?)
Deny the Universe in me?
  Well tell me, where does Cosmos end?
Space-Time is warped, and other 'Me's'
  Exist in atoms of my own.
Space-Time? Oh yes but more
  Than this, another Star to call our own,
A stellar system, still denied
  On micro, micro-cosmic scale,
Particles of life and structure,
  Universes in a cell.
A Cosmic Colosseum, in scale
  That has no Earthly parallel.

18 POINT 7 BILLION

Every solid artefact on Earth
   He says,
Is 99.9 percent
   Emptiness.
Thus only one percent
   (Or less)
Can actually exist.
   Which makes illusion of
The rest.

Equally profound,
   Mayfly lives its four-score and ten
Within the span
   Of my one
Earthly day.

Do angels dance on a needle's point?
   Why 'Yes,
Yes,'
   For 99 percent is space
And all the rest
   Concentrated, in collapsed
Atomic nuclei.

But this requires that God and Man
   Combine in vain collusion.
Such certainty betrays
   The folly of our days
When arrogant
   Man
Looks for Universal beginning,
   A pencil-point to trace The Plan
Of God's infinity,

  Eighteen-point-seven
Billion years
  Ago.
Far too much to contemplate,

Except the proud sophisticate
  Able thus to calculate
To point seven billion – not point eight!
  Without the question,
'Wait!
  What was there,
There?
  Before it all began?'
Another seed,
  A time or place
From which
  Eventually, there sprang
The human race.

For who can challenge such a dot
  When science says 'X' marks the spot
And all Creation starts from here.
  Before I claim such knowledge
As a fact
  I do fear
Equality with God!
  18 point 7 billion?
Such certainty
  Has no place here.

THE PROTECTIVE VEIL

Science is the protective veil
Drawn over the fragile web of Faith,
For I believe, as Saints and Galahad
Believed.
And the serenity of unresolved
Knowledge
Is the Holy Grail of
Revelation.
For blind science is a mere
Path of questions,
Each answer leading to
A receding
Never to be revealed,
Truth,
Known only in the deep
Intensity of Faith.
And Certain knowledge,
No matter what I learn,
Seeks only to
Confirm
In truth, I know nothing
At all.

THE LIFE WE ASPIRE TO, THE LIFE THAT WE LEAD

These are the girls, tossing and preening
Their wonderful hair,
Shining and gleaming
Smiling the smile that we others are dreaming

Of love and success, life lived to excess,
With never a sign of anxiety, stress.
So I buy what she says
For we're worth it these days,
And try to forget that I'm drudgery's slave.
But somehow for me it doesn't hang true,
After hours in the glass
I still wouldn't pass.
For the promise denies
(with its unspoken lies)
A simple reality
I can't disguise.
Tho' I'm dying to try,
And trying to dye
I look with despair and turn with a sigh
From the girl on the screen
Who is peddling the dream
That with her little bottle
I'm every man's queen.
And so with despair
As I look at my hair
I decide it's the shape,
The wrong cut at the nape
That denies me
And tries me,
And I can't escape!
So I sit in my sox
With some consoling chox
And try not to envy the girl on the box
For I know I'm not perfect,
Their world is a sham,
And tho' I know I'm worth it
I don't give a damn!

PERFORMANCE 4

ENGLISH ABOVE ALL
(2012)

Above all I am English!
For there lives in me an expression of the past
Flourishing in sounds and memories.
Those I loved still live
Within me – smiling
Bustling in their world,
A world I knew, a world I shared.
I will not be ashamed, not when
Decencies abound from ages lost,
Inherited from those I never knew;
Whose influence, potent and profound
Gave to me my disciplines.
And so I will not denigrate
Nor faithlessly forsake
My past, a dream come real,
Rooted in England,
Reflected not in the warrior zeal
Of heroes – though yes – there are a few –
But in the sights and sounds of landscape,
Lyrical and potent like music, an ideal.
The faint chorale of English hymns
Heard through the soft glow of windows;
Strangely reassuring,
A comfort in the fading russet light of autumn.
Images of England rising,
Uncompromising white
From the shingled Narrow Sea;
Or staring east across ancient kingdoms,
Farm and fen – Mercia –
Rich in peasant history,
Unfettered in her view from Malvern,
Over troubled Europe
To Russia's mighty Urals.

A land rich in design blessed
By generations of artistic artisans,
Unafraid, generous, boisterous,
Peaceful, kind
And oh! – so vulnerable with her gifts
Of freedom.
More than myth, Englishness is tangible and real;
A land arising from her past,
An England only Englishmen can feel.

REQUIEM

Oh where is love, the plaintive song
   Sung by the old, sung to the young?
A song of sadness, a song of hope
   For all the life that lies before
Your tender years, this is my song.
   Such things to tell of, things to see
And dreams to live with high ideals;
   My songs are of what might have been
When I was young and had my dream,
   And revelation's mighty voice
Came whispering in the night.
   I have a song.

My song is wisdom, the wisdom of years
   That echoes in silence and dwells in my heart;
Tempered by Love and quenched in my Fears.
   My song was born when Hope was high
And life a dream of pure ideals;
   I turn and see myself in thee.

For a child is a seer, a child is a sage

   And all life's knowledge is learned
At this age.
   But tho' knowledge and wisdom reside in a child
Learning from Age cannot be reconciled.
   My knowledge and learning, so carefully hoarded
Must now be laid aside, discarded!
   Life's lessons I place at your feet in vain,
For your eyes have the look of a child's disdain.

But someday children in your futures
   You will be my sad today.
Will you bequeath the Utopia I dreamed,
   The Summer of Love, the high ideal?
Will you have made dreams of your own come real?

Oh my dear child with heart unsullied,
   So generous and filled with song,
I yearn to pass my dreams to you,
   The dreams we had when I was young.
But you will let them pass unspoken,
   Resonating in your head
'Till in your heart, just as in mine
   The rhythm of life's last song will chime,
'I have a song,
   A song of truth
        I used to hear when but a youth,
I song I yearn to hear again…'
   You listen for my song in vain.

LET'S FACE REALITY

No more the morning; break of day
  Is meaningless, time does not stay.
The year's at nought
  And nothing that your life has bought
Has meaning!
  Days spent straining, scheming, dreaming;
Projects that once loomed so large
  Are meaningless on Chiron's barge.
Where is true friendship?
  Where is it found
Amongst the people all around?
  I have my palace and my treasure;
Enough excitements for my leisure –
  Beauty of the human kind,
All I want, desire or need
  Within the world
Is mine!
  Servants and my sycophants,
Everything indulgence grants except –
  I'm running out of time!
And they are running too.
  Not friends, not friends
For I don't know what friendship is,
  And now the people who surrounded me
Are hounding me,
  Reclaiming favours, obligations;
All I have the power to grant
  But still,
I have not the will
  To grant false fleeting parasites
Their old insatiable appetites
  To fill.
And so they wait; they wait in vain,
  For I have seen

The dusky shadow,
  Imperfect – like a dream
Chiron in his barge
  Waiting to convey,
To take me on my final, lonely way
  Without a friend!
Such is the end.

EDEN RE-VISITED, EDEN REVILED

Ah, the Earthly Paradise,
  The dream that dwelt in Gospel's fable;
All things given,
  Nothing wanting
In the garden
  At God's table
Under heaven's benign sky,
  Eve and Adam, you and I.
Until (to foster wanton discontent)
  A serpent armed with guile was sent
To Eve, and she – the fable goes –
  In nakedness felt shame.
The serpent smiled
  And Man, by God reviled
Was banished
  Like an unrepentant child.
A moral fable this, told with soft indulgence
  Save - ? - ?
Time has no meaning in the conscious dream
  And things that were, are now no longer seen
As once portrayed,
  Vague,
        Comforting,
                Serene.

This is no fable from
        The innocence of man,
A story of how mankind began!
        This is no dream
But prophesy!
        In Eden now we are despoiling
Paradise, worshipping the Holy Cow
        Of self-indulgent greed!
This is no dream
        Of things that might have been,
For daily Paradise retreats,
        Replaced by fetid, squalid streets;
The burgeoning poor clamouring at
        Heaven's door
While Eden shrinks.
        And all around the plundered Earth's
Reduced to barren ground.
        The legend, fond and harmless
From the past is yet to be fulfilled
        I God's forthcoming blast!

OH MY DEAR CHILD
(2002)

Oh my dear child, son of my son
  Whose life is scarcely yet begun,
Who gazes with such trusting eyes
  Upon the world,
Your days-to-come are scarce unfurled.
  The secrets of the days ahead –
Your dreams – unfold within your bed.
  Sleep, sweet my child,
Safe, snug within your blankets curled.
  My tears, the tears that fall are not for me

For I have known a jewelled world
   And I have heard its joyous song,
And breathed its fragrance all life long.
   And I have known ambition's spur
And shared my life in love with Her
   You know and love, child of my child.
And this I'd share and pass to you;
   The joy of Earth, the love of Life,
The splendour that was once so rife.
   But now I gaze through melting tears
At future's doubt with mounting fears.
   You cannot know a life like mine
(Tho' would that I could re-call time
   And give to you
The world I knew)
   But, of the future what do I see?
I wish I could bequeath to thee
   The world.
Oh such a world of leisure,
   Pleasure,
Work and just reward.
   A world once big enough to share;
A world now shrunk, by man depleted,
   Deserts where a lake retreated,
Nomads on an arid plain,
   Dust clouds where there once was rain!
But the privileged and wealthy
   In their shrinking world of plenty
Think they're ruling but they're failing,
   While around the sound of wailing
'Till the writhing, dying mass
   Falls like locusts on the grass.
All these things will come to pass
   While the selfish Lords of Plenty
Are left ruling what is empty,
   Just a hollow, dying ember.

I remember, I remember
  All the things it used to be.
And oh! – my dear, my darling child,
  I wish that I could pass to thee
The world that was bequeathed to me.

EARTH MOTHER

'You are killing me!'
The last despairing, soft protest,
A sigh,
Remains unheard
By
The jostling, gasping,
Groping, sucking,
Greedy, gulping herd,
Without a care
For how and where.
While exhausted, unreplenished
She lies crying,
Helpless, dying.
And still unheeding,
Swarming from her womb they're teeming;
Digging, chewing,
Sucking, seeking…
But barren Mother has
No more to give
And so the host, with no means left to feed
Turns upon itself
In final, frenzied greed!

ELEGY IN A COUNTRY CARPARK
(Written in support of Ledbury's opposition to Tesco)
(2011)

No curfew tolls the knell of closing day
      As juggernaut climbs slowly o'er the lea,
The dimming down of twinkling high street shops
      Leaves Ledbury to darkness and to me.

Well, who'd object to wealth and healthy profit?
      Who'd be a Luddite to defend the few?
Why ever would you want to cry out, 'Stop it!'
      When benefits are certain to accrue?

The siren lure of wealth and job creation,
      Soft promises, inducements to the few,
The altruistic gifts they give the nation
      Impoverish the town – that's me and you!

A patriot's flagpoles, windows double glazed,
      Are deemed to scandalise sweet Ledbury's dream,
But mammoth corporations on the skyline
      Are neither deemed obtrusive nor obscene!

The pretty high street with its wealth of shops,
      The citizens who patronise them all,
Will find their fellows struggling and failing
      When varied choice is held in mammon's thrall.

The richness of our heritage and culture
      Is given scant concern when all the plans
Submitted by the obscene bloated vulture
      Are scrutinised and passed from hand-to-hand.

How drab the prospect, oh! - how drear the future
    When lifeless empty windows face the street,
And shoppers footsteps turn to the invader –
    Sainsbury's with whom their fellows can't compete!

For all the riches promised, the enhancement
    Of shopping and the visitors to town,
Are nothing when such high street dereliction
    Is Tesco's dreadful legacy to hand down

The corner shop, familiar village store,
    The friendly, smiling faces as you enter
Are banished to the checkout's trilling call;
    So sad, a high street robbed of private venture.

Farewell the livelihood of generations,
    The old familiar faces on the street
Thus ousted from tradition's family stations
    To make the gorging monsters more replete.

THE SHEPHERD'S WHEEL
(A restored 18th C millwheel and forge in the western suburbs of Sheffield)

i - Down Porter Brook
Below the bank, a hillside rank
With trees, the mud-lined stream.
Decaying leaves in small islands rise
From black, rotten debris
Carried deep and slow on porter's scale.
This is no Wye, this rippling stream,
Rising on Plynlimon;
No salmon leap for sport, no bends reveal
Castle crags and swirling entry to Sabrina and
The sea.

This tributary Porter, running to
The Don;
A shallow, shaded rivulet is winding
Between moss and fern,
Over stones and secret rills
And narrow, stone lined channels
To lethargic ponds
Where audacious ducks waddle,
And leaf-choked sluices
Leak waterfalls and sprays back into the stream.
But this stream has memories…

ii – The Factory
Far beyond the wooded bank,
High above on Hope's high moor,
Scoured by Pennine's ceaseless breeze
Where curlews call and scattered sheep
Follow hidden bracken paths
Below the broken line of broken crags,
A factory; open, cold and bare,
Where sculptors work, out in the air.
No lavish, floral columns rise
In silhouette against the skies;
Nor abbey, futile atonement
For the murder of a priest,
With pilgrims streaming and stained glass
Gleaming in the sunrise from the East.
Only wheels!
Carved with more perfection
Than Gothic symbols
Reaching up in praise;
Just gritstone wheels, shepherd's wheels,
Lumbering in careful cavalcade
To Porter Brook
A league or so away.

iii - The little mester
Above the call of birdsong in the trees
Hear the rumble of the wheels,
Turning with inexorable power.
Astride the bench the man,
A coughing, spitting artisan
Crouched close, holding down the blade,
Is drawing steel against the stone.
His dialect coarse and warm,
Drawn from uncouth Sheffield,
A confident long-vowelled sound,
In rasping, choking dust is drowned
By sparkling grit and steel
Rising from the mighty stone;
Driven by the creaking, clicking
Groaning paddle-wheel.
And from the paddles flows,
Unheard, the plash of water
Leaving soft, a sparkling rainbow
Of fairy-light above the spilling Porter.
In killing sparks the craftsman's artefact is made;
A thing of beauty, a craftsman's tool,
A Sheffield blade
Forged, honed and polished by
Little Mesters
At Porter Brook, on Shepherd's Wheel.

iv – Epilogue
The water flows. This gentle stream
Won't seize the mind with wonderment
Or gasps of awe. No mighty river this,
Only the modest fore-runner of tomorrow's dream;
Generator of power from simple re-used waters
And gritstone wheels,
Feeding infant industry with undiminished energy
'Till the infant became full-grown

With industrial might downstream
And Porter's workshops died,
Were swept away.
Now only silted pond-beds stay,
And tiny, black dead leaves slowly drift
On lazy eddies, in silence unbroken.
No memories are spoken;
No echo rises from the rasp of gritstone on the blade
To show how from modest, rippling Porter
England's might was made.

IN THE TRENCHES

This is my home; a bank of earth,
A muddy shelf, a mug, a brush,
A photograph of those I love.
This is my home whilst what I dream
Is far away, too long unseen;
The homely scent, a mother's arms,
And shy, demure, another's charms.
She whom I love and who I miss;
The tenderness, the loving kiss.
She smiles at me, a sepia smile
That breaks my heart
Whilst waiting for the guns to start.

WE TWO

Now has come the time to share the pleasures of romance
That only comes through years of love,
And the constancy of love's devotion,
Sustained even whilst sailing through life's
Sometime stormy ocean while we seek
Calm waters, a haven, sleep.
Contentment, safe from the raging of the deep…
Ah! – Love's sublime treasured moments that outweigh
Things mundane, the irritations of
Another day.
Rare instances, intense tho' fleeting,
These are the memories that stay:
Friendship re-kindled with delight;
The warmth of unsought kindness,
But more than this,
The sheer exalting pleasure of the unexpected kiss,
So filled with love
Like the inexperienced kiss of love, remembered
After many years. Let not romance die!
I still see pleasure and approval shine
From your appraising eye.
Shall I explain? If you cannot guess
No deal of explanation will reveal
The How? – Or Why? Only these:
A hotel window overlooking Chestnut trees,
Lake Konstanze, Switzerland's shore in gleaming
Distant light and my love with me,
Receiving? - nothing much
But in her hand I pressed
A bowl of cherries (wrapped in paper)
And envious glances from among the rest.
Morning moonlight, a mountain
Seen from an Alpine balcony, a castle
Gleaming under the stars

And my beloved, kissed, enfolded in my arms.
Dancing, alone in the ballroom while
The approving band plays on
For just we two.
Thoughts, memories, happy sounds
Jostling in my mind, each treasured moment
Seeking recognition in a look,
A remembered dart of love
So overwhelming that years exist no more,
Just we two, the way we are,
The way we were before.

LOVE'S JOYS RE-CALLED
(August 2014)

Listen! – from the innocence of childhood
Memories spring.
They cannot fade
But live and breath
In everything.

And from the shade
That sometimes darkens passing days
Behold! –
Love's joys recalled creep joyful,
Like a fairy from a glade.

Ah my lovely Jude
We have a lifetime of Love
Between us.

Happy, Happy Birthday

LOVE'S DREAM

How shall I describe the joy
My lady's love brings to my life,
The ladylove who is my wife?
She is the sweet fulfilment of content,
Sweeping love's oblivion through my senses,
Rapturous, eternal and unseen
When passion's spent.

How can I recapture when
No teasing, haunting scent is there?
Only some thing, undefined;
A touch, the fleeting, fading memory of a kiss,
A strand of hair.

Love is not of the world.
Futile to seek the worldly substance of a dream
That lingers and is gone.
Love, a dream that lives within the mind,
Transcends all slights and failures,
The cruelty of mankind.
But Oh! – the touch of love's sweet memory;
Hand-in-hand, heart-to-heart,
Loved and loving
Soaring across Love's Universe with joy.

WHAT A DIFFERENCE A DAY MAKES

Back in the madness,
The 10th of November
I killed you, my enemy,
Well I remember!
But now a day later

   I greet you as friend,
I'm told not to hate
   Now the war's at an end.
But what of the people
   Who soured my emotions
And sent me away
   From my loved one's devotions
And taught me despite my beliefs,
   Like all fools –
That war had a purpose,
   With honour and rules.
And still rules? Who rules?
   Tell me the rule that says
Napalm is good;
   Or the rule that absolved me
As frenzied I stood
   And poured burning kerosene into a trench
(I still hear their screams; still carry their stench).
   As I cling to my honour, and remnants of pride
In those who marched with me,
   Who fought by my side.
For the horror remains,
   My soul's sullied and stain'd
And the mem'ries live on
   In my tormented brain.
Is this what I fought for?
   Well, I was deceived
For the reason they gave
   Wasn't what I believed.

I BELIEVE

I believe in heaven.
I believe in the presence that looks
With Benevolence
From that place
Beyond the finite measurement of Space
And stellar years,
And the quantum span of time to
Galaxies, nebulous and far
Beyond the farthest gleaming star.
I believe in Heaven.

I believe in the Divine
Existing in a different element of time,
Untrammelled by
The brevity of man;
The shrivelled wisdom of an Earthly span.
For heaven – I have you know –
Is near not far;
Far closer than the nearest distant star;
Unreachable, unseen, and closer
Than a vague remembered dream;
A sound Divine.

I know
That each of us has heard
The truth of life
Revealed in the unspoken Word.

SWEET MEMORY'S SONG

I feel the shadow of encroaching age,
The fear that life is rushing by
In years of love I'd love to live again.
Instead I live surrounded by life's 'things'
While 'things' I yearn for are denied;
Yes – even love's sharp counterbalance – pain.
In childhood's (and my children's) day,
Sweet memories live; are lost in play;
The friendships gained and friendships lost.
We never knew we'd lose each other
And ourselves.
The faces fade;
The treasured friends' approving smiles;
And now I can't recall them back
To justify, to understand
What were my faults?
Were they so grand, so great
That friendship died?
But was it simply death alone
That took them from my side?
The living mingle with the dead,
And others? – well, who knows?
I wish them peace,
The peace I still seek for myself.
No matter, I wish no man ill.
But how I wish that I could see them still.

I yearn for what is now unseen -
Though what was lost did not exist -
Just folklore, part of England's dream
Like day perceived through morning's mist.
And memory sets my heart to yearning -
To live again youth's Golden Age,
Despite the lessons of life's learning –

The scenes my heartache can't assuage.
Oh was there ever such an age?

So now the comfort of my years
Is spent with shadows from my past,
But memories fade; truth disappears,
And false contentment comes at last.
Perhaps you weep, perhaps you sigh
And try to speak, to say 'goodbye';
A kind of comfort's what you seek
Casting for mem'ries in the sky.
While all around, as people throng
You long to hear sweet memory's song.

TO FRIENDS

... for friendship is a treasure
  Which you cannot see or store
Friendship gives before requesting
        For itself, - and what is more
All it asks is that you think of me
        Just as I've thought of you
When I've shared your pain or sorrow
        (just as all good friends would do).
And there's mem'ries too of happiness
        In place of stress or strife
In the sounds of someone laughing.
        Friendship soothes away the burdens
And brings meaning back to life.

Yes, life's treasure is in friendship,
        Which you cannot count or store;
Simply undefined within the mind

It's 'goodness' – nothing more.

Ah! the golden gift of friendship
    Is the gift we treasure most
Of the gifts bestowed upon us
    By our Hostess and our Host,
And that's what we remember
    As we honour them today,
The simple generosity
    Of Rosemary and Ray.

MEMORY'S HERITAGE

Bright cobbles gleam, I walk the street,
Wet sandstone flagstones at my feet,
Dark sooty walls on either side;
At faceless windows watchers hide;
Suspicion bars each silent door
Where lurk the nervous, hopeless poor.
No altruistic spirit fills
The hearts of those who bear life's ills.

Along the dark remembered streets,
    Behind the brick façade,
Lurk fragments, ghosts of comradeship
    Within the hidden yard;
Familiar, faceless, welcome, warm,
    But comradeship was hard.

Ah golden days, remembered days,
The days when we were young,
Days passed secure in happiness,
That's how our life was sung.
The heart-of-gold, a mother's hug;

Adversity o'ercome by love.

And mem'ries, dreams of what might be,
What we might have become,
Are twisted in reality,
Not in the dreams of home.
No-one can face the past's grim truth
Of who was me and who was her,
The cruelties and pettiness
. Of how it was and who we were.

Millennia have shown the way
And I will testify today
That here,
'twixt Faith and faithless Hell,
We could have been as angels;
But Paradise was plundered;
By brutal greed and misplaced guilt
Our dreams were torn and sundered.

I hate the dark; the fearful dark,
Of all embracing night,
No starbright clouds against the moon,
Nor silver wings in flight;
Or daisies faint across the lawn,
Against the forest's loom
Like star-sky, shimmering bright.
My dark the fearful ghost-train dark
Of unknown startling fears;
The infinite, the unplumbed depth,
The dark beneath the stairs;
Deep within my mind
Tortured by the unredeemed
Unkindness of mankind.

I WILL; I DO
(The wedding of our granddaughter, June 21ˢᵗ 2013)

"And will you place your hand in mine,
And love me now as I love you?
And love me Ricky, through all time,
In winter, summer, all year through?"

"Oh Danii yes, I will, I do."

"And yes dear Ricky, I will too.
For I have loved you from the start,
That day you came and stole my heart."

**"And on that day that changed our lives
I vowed to keep you by my side,
To be your husband; you my bride.
So Danii this Midsummer's day
As I pledge you my love, my life;
Will you consent to be my wife?"**

"Oh Ricky yes, I will, I do."

ON 'JUDY-LOO' AT SEVENTY-TWO
(2013)

Come with me and be my Queen
And let us travel all serene
Through this and every passing day;
Let pleasure keep mundane at bay,
For life is made for joy and Love
And this together we will prove.
So come with me my lovely Queen,
Your birthday beckons, live the Dream!

BILLY
('Walkies!' for a little white Westie)

Scents and odours fill the air;
Borne on breezes, lingers, teases
This way that way,
Back and forth,
Searching through the undergrowth,
Sniffing – who was there before?
Leave my mark (a recognition;
Me! - For when she comes again)
He tugs my leash, I have to strain.
There's a rustle in the leaves,
A whirr of wings high in the trees
And fluttering, chattering; sounds that tease;
I stand alert, held on the leash.

How soon the freedom ends
(If 'freedom'
Is the name to give!)
When all I do is strain
To dash, to turn, to chase…?
Instead we turn for home again.

BIRTHSONG

I was born when the moon was weeping
And my mother gave birth in blood.
While around all the world was sleeping,
And nobody understood
And she took her bundle, and wiped his eyes
As her echoing agony fades and dies,
Subsumed in the waking infant's cries
And she laid him aside.

And the child grew and sought his tomorrow,
Filling his years in play;
While the golden Apollo
Shone down in sorrow
On the mother's weeping day.
And as shadows encroached
The ravens approached
And picked at the entrails that lay;
At the strife;
At her life.

For she'd dreamed of a new beginning,
She had hoped for a morning-bright start;
But the world looked askance
And denied her the dance;
And the rhythm of loveliness,
Peace and esteem
Retreated before in
Another man's dream.
All hope of redemption
Washed out in the stream
Of events.
For the child she bore she rejected;
Their kisses were torn asunder,
For neither was protected

From the rampage and the plunder
That tore at her heart
As they pulled them apart
With indifferent eyes.
'I'm his mother!' she cried
But her love was denied.
'Don't forsook me!' she pleaded,
'You know how I tried!!'
But too late to make good
She remained where she stood;
Between them a gulf
Bridged with hate,
Filled with blood.

But a mother is always a mother,
And a child can never escape.
Tho' the memories they're trying to smother
(The look so mild she bestowed on her child)
Are denied as obscene
(They're not what they seem).
So the world turned and left her
Rejected, reviled;
This maid, once a mother, bereft of her child.
Did she wonder a little or often;
Was love ever there? Could time not repair?
Did memory never soften?
Did she gaze into emptiness
Wishing me there?

Tho' the moon may cease it's weeping
Over our fretful sleep,
The sunlight gives birth
To shadows on earth;
In the landscape of life,
Through contentment and strife
Our destiny's all we're entrusted to keep.

SEPTEMBER DREAMS

The summer's over though the days still shine
   And borders shimmer; regal colours
In sunlight's golden radiance of love.
   And yet bold summer's patterns have
A faded look – not less bright but -
   Less responsive to the cooling light.

Summer's past; long, languid days remembered.
   Images old, and new-gone bring
The warmth of love, uncritical and bright,
   And slumber's ease in soft untroubled night.
Friends reappear, live on; their smiles
   Undimmed in memory's fast receding miles.

Days tempered in the freshness of the wind.
   Beyond the harvest, swallows sensing home
Wheel from dawn to sudden unexpected dusk.
   Ah! Saint Luke's final welcome autumn haze,
'till gusts of swirling leaves replace memories
   Of sunlit days in the cold indifference of rain.

Winter, cold, relentless sweeps upon us,
   With no remorse the wind, increasing, gusts.
Cold days darken brooding moods; depression
   Adds its weight to winter's strain.
And meanwhile, sleeping undisturbed beneath us
   Earth mother sleeps until re-born again.

THE SPIRIT LIVES ON
(After Betjeman)
(2012)

Try not to talk to the neighbours dear,
It's not that I'm being a snob
But the last line of washing's been out there for days
And I'm certain he hasn't a job.

It's not that we think they're inferior to us,
Or not from the same social class;
But they don't seem to have no refinement
(when she speaks it's the bray of an ass!)

And she thinks she's a stunner, he thinks he's a stud
So the children don't know any better.
She parades in such outfits while he's such a slob;
And there's holes in the youngest child's sweater!

It's really quite taxing to keep up one's end
Against such insuperable odds;
I'm sure all the neighbours (if you were to ask)
Would say we've got standards, not snobs.

For in this day-and-age it's almost a crime
To drift by with one's standards so low.
I don't wish them ill, if they'd only improve;
Or failing that, why don't they go!

THE MISSION

'We are lovers of peace', he declared to the world
While above him the banners of war were unfurled
Yet again!
For the 'insult' or 'incident' has set in train
The 'measured response'
(diplomatic, of course)
Of indignant self-righteousness.
Protest's in vain
As the dogs are unleashed
In the valley of peace.

Protest for what?
To unsay a word? To unthink a thought?
To suppress an ideal that is
Only made real by the
Fear and uncertainty all of us feel?

For every new 'leader' must have his own war
(Though no-one knows why or what it is for)
Except it's a way of placating the mob
Around him who say 'He's no good at his job.'
So with stout declarations and ringing intent
(Saying all other options pursued have been spent)
The leader displays both reluctance and zeal
And hopes we will all understand him and feel
That 'the mission', 'objective', the 'what it is for'
Will placate and convince us in going to war.

A MOMENT'S HESITATION

He remembered as a clean-limbed boy, standing
By the water's edge, hesitant, not wanting to appear
A fool.
The water clear and still within the pool,
Inviting, cool.
A moment's hesitation.
Fatal.
So he numbed his mind
And thought instead
Of water coursing o'er his limbs
And dived straight in.
Shock!
And then (he had known all along)
Breaking the surface in spray
And laughing with a small head-wave.
He wasn't brave.
But it took a kind of courage to be first!

Now here he was again,
Trying to re-create the numbing of his brain
Before the plunge.
Not a dive; not this time but
A fearful thrust above the earth,
To lunge beneath the wire,
Anticipating rifle and machine-gun fire.
Close the mind, obliterate the fear;
Don't run but show
How easy, though so slow,
How far it is to walk.

He sensed his comrades
Stumbling; heard their yelps
Until he felt

Quite alone.
Others distant like him, walking,
Ever thinning, a slowing tide,
Until he reached the other side
And made them prisoners,
(The three who manned the gun).
Chatting, happy, waiting for the
Remnants of his comrades
Finally to come.
'VC at least' they cried but he,
Beyond euphoria,
Evaded all their chorus of applause,
Suddenly appalled
By what he'd done.

What might have been!
Became the substance of
A sad recurring dream.
He'd seen
The foolish limit of his life.
And though he'd never heard the sound,
His waking memory was racked
By whirr and whine
Of bullets, the awful thud
As comrades bodies
Hit the ground
And subversive fear began to hammer at his brain.
How could he walk that way again,
Go through another such horrific
Waking, dying day?

Once more the order came.

Too much memory!
He braced and sought to find
The numbness; breathing calm

As if beside the pool he'd left behind,
But, awful anticipation entering
His mind
He trembled, and the look,
The awful
Vacant look of fear
Transmuted images in eyes
They could not recognise,
Hearing only soft unstifled sobs until
The whistle!
And they turned, all around
His comrades, scrambling up,
And stumbling, staggering, grotesque,
Killed and wounded
On the ground.

Pushed, pulled, threatened, abused, he had no will
To go out with the rest to kill.
But heroism had no credit in its store
Nor recognised what he had done before.
Only 'Coward' pinned on paper to his breast.
And now he remembered
As it was; a clean-limbed boy.
Only now,
Erect against the pole.
He sought refuge in memory;
The anticipation of the first
Cold shock of water
Coursing over skin,
Bursting up in spray into the air
And smiled an uncomprehending smile
As the bullets he'd so feared
Released him from his dreams.

MEMORIAL
(So many Memorials lining the path beneath the trees to Walford village Church)

A brief Remembrance of each beating heart,
Beating with Love so far away;
Trusting with hope and stern belief
'till the fated telegram is received.
Only the carved memorials remain
Beneath trees haunted
By memories
Of him, and other men…

LOVE'S DIALOGUE

Give me your hand, your yearning hand,
  Let your palm rest in mine;
Let gentle, tender fingertips
  Speak 'Love' and soft entwine.

Give me your heart, your lonely heart,
  For my heart lives in thine;
Return my heart, return my Love
  Just as I give thee mine.

Give me your life, come live with me
  And do not count the time.
I have no life without your Love
  And I have pledged thee mine.

THE DEEP

Deeper; deeper in the darkness,
In the darkness of my mind;
Lost in memory's deep recesses
Are events we left behind,
As from the fathoms of the ocean
(where things lurk but can't be seen)
Rising out of swirling currents
Come the fragments of the dream.

LOVE DIVINED?

It isn't, 'How do I love thee?'
  Whispered in melting passion past,
For love's an all-consuming fire,
  Fanned deeper than emotion's blast.
My Love transcends the day-to-day,
  The lingering, ardent gaze;
Love casts the mundane life away,
  And dominates my days.
Romance, Dear Jude fulfils my life
  Because I have you for my wife.

SPEED ME ON MY JOURNEY

Speed me on my journey,
Send me on my way with Love;
Sing for me. For I am going
To the threshold of Heaven,
A place I know, to wait
In an eternity of love and peace.

And I will watch you from the clouds
And smile on you in starlight,
And send the warmth of everlasting Love
When life becomes too hard to bear.
For I have never left you,
And I will still protect you,
And there at heaven's door I'll wait
Until you join me there.

ON RAINBOW HILL
(2013)

I came to see you yesterday,
  Lingered in silence 'neath your trees;
You could not know, nor could you hear
  Me as I stood and shared your peace

While mem'ries all about me rose.
  Earth scents of childhood in the haze
Caressing like a healing balm; your
  Smile appears - and fleeting - fades.

Sounds borne on shimmering Malvern's breeze;
  A dove's repeated soft refrain;

A churchbell chimes; down Rainbow Hill
Faint whistle of a leaving train.

The memories pass relentless on;
  Sweet pangs of love and lingering pain;
Life's past! - I must depart whilst here
  In childhood's dreams you must remain.

FOR AUDREY
(On being 90 - 12th June 2015)

Life, like a fond remembered stream
Flows on; in swirls and eddies
Memories rise unbidden from the deep;
Caught sometimes by a scent, or sounds
Of laughter heard in
Life's contented sleep.

But mem'ry is no mask of past regret
When recollections of
Times spent in love arise,
And love's pure light still shines
And twinkles in her eyes.
Ah Love;
Of all life's passions
Love is life's great prize.

And yet, beyond the sound of laughter
Do tears of sadness
For love lost arise?
No!
For from her heart
Defiant, Audrey cries,
'I will not be a hermit

To dwell within a cave,
But each day wake afresh
And try to misbehave!'

And still life brings rewards;
(It need not bestow loneliness and fears)
Lo! See the miracle of friends
Who come to love, and with that love, respect
The steadfastness of Audrey's friendship through the years.

Life's gentle stream flows on;
Fond memory cannot tarnish or congeal
When memories new conspire to make amends
And Audrey's impish twinkle makes love real.

So let us share her laughter, see her smile,
And here today with Audrey
Enjoy each other's company awhile.

I LOVE YOU

I love you more than 'Question Time',
    I love you more than shopping.
I love you more than springtime
    Or when summer rain is dropping.
I love you when the night falls;
    I love you when it's light.
I love you in the morning
    As I've loved you through the night.
I love you when your look at me
    Makes thoughts run through my head.
I love you hidden in the woods
    And love you in our bed.
I've loved you since I met you;

Through our years of married life.
I love you Jude, for loving me,
My darling loving wife.

LIFE'S REMEMBERED LOVE
(Christmas 2014)

I recall an instant years ago;
Our two eyes shyly met;
And as sunlight melts snow on slopes
My life became renewed with hopes.

And so when our two hearts entwined
Our lives became as one;
Bound together – it cannot be denied –
Even before you were my bride.

And I have loved each moment
Of the life we two have shared.
And still I hear you gently say, 'I love you.'
Yes! – You've loved me, this I know;
You told me so each day.

And I've loved you, I hope you know
With Love such as no lady ever was before;
And pledge again, this Christmas Day,
'I love you Jude.'
My darling wife, I'll love you evermore

I HAVEN'T CEASED…
(2014)

I haven't ceased to be
Because I'm seventy-three,
And cannot bend to tie my shoe
And do the things I used to do.

In heart I'm just the same;
In spirit my one aim
Is still to stand and take my place
And do my best to win my race!

So don't cast me aside;
I still retain my pride,
'cos I've done things you've yet to try,
And I'll do more yet 'ere I die!

BIG BANG

Did you think I would allow you
   The infinity of wisdom?
Did you think I'd trust mankind
   With the secrets of my mind?
What you took from Me in Eden
   (by theft, triggered by deceit)
Wasn't what I planned to offer you
   And place before your feet.
By taking what I might bestow
   You presumed upon My gift.
Your avaricious weakness
   Was the reason for the rift.

Now you stumble in blind arrogance,

Seek knowledge and seek power
And I watch with resignation
　As you build a Babel's Tower.
For I see no sign of unity,
　Just arrogance and greed
While you leave the poor in poverty
　And blame them for their need
With sophisticated conversation
　That's designed to feed
Your own self-serving selfishness
　That poisons mankind's seed.

So the Gift I might have given you
　I'm glad that I withhold;
You are too rash and too unkind,
　Too reckless and too bold.
You cannot grasp Infinity
　Of Universe or Me
Can't see beyond the limits
　That I set into the Tree.
For nothing has real Power
　Or the Wisdom except Me.
It started with a Bang! You say,
　Creation's mighty roar.
You pygmy intellect; Mankind
　You fail until you have divine
What must have been before!

St. SWITHIN 1991

I write the verse of war
And the romance of the dead.
40 days and 40 nights,
For 40 days it rained

Bombs and shells and missiles
(Not an inch of ground was gained).

War without death
Was the war that we read
In the news as reported
(not 400 dead).
'We don't kill civilians!'
Rules of Engagement said.
But a missile down an air-vent
Killed more in a 'US strike'.
Somebody knew. But who, but who?
The child of war is the lie, the lie!
When missiles rain down from the sky!

THE BIRDS AND THE BEES

Trap the birds, kill the bees;
Bring the country to its knees,
Take the music from the skies,
Take the pleasure from our eyes.
Here is nature's rule of thumb;
Mankind dies when bees don't hum!

THE ANGEL

The sweet quiet streets in which we used to play
And pursue our mind's adventures day by happy day…
Are missed,
Forgotten, gone.
… and seeing my child-helpless plight,
Alone, distressed in the night
The angel with unfolding wings, stirred
And spread them, casting light
Where shadows held the fears
The child tried vainly to forbid.
And he settled, blessed in brief content.

But now those days are gone.
The breathing, living, sweating striving
Avaricious world moves on.
With give-and-taking.
And Angels, dismissed, remote as
Heaven's Star,
See, sometimes,
The frailty of mankind,
Neglectful of the childlike faith that's
Left behind.
And the angel folds his wings…

DOG-EAT-DOG

There are those who will reach out and take
From the hands of the others who need.
There will always be those 'on the make',
Shameless and driven by greed.
And the world was always thus,

With the 'haves' sneering at the 'have-nots';
Who think of themselves
As a species superior
With never a care for all those inferior;
The down on their luck, the down on their knees
Down in the mouth, down in the gutter
Whose protest (inadequate) is barely a stutter,
Unheard.

Let me ask you why should it be so?
Has compassion fallen so low
That the weak, cast aside have their poverty denied
While the glittering world of arrogant pride
Brutally, callously sneer (passing wide)
'You think you're owed a living!'
But would never think of giving
To alleviate the poor,
Where desperation beats their door.

THE DARK

Hate the dark; be fearful of the dark,
The ghost-train dark of unknown,
Trailing, startling fears.
Not friendly dark of all embracing night,
The dark of bright-edged clouds against the moon,
Or silver silhouetted things in flight
Against the darker forest's loom.
Or daisies like a star-sky,
Dimly bright across the lawn.
My dark is deeper than
The dark beneath the stairs;
The infinity of dark
Within my mind;

Tortured by the unredeemed
Depravity of
Humankind.
We could be as angels
For millennia have shown the way
Except that we are what we are
And have been, and continue so,
Today.

LOVE'S RIDDLE

Who is she who breathes
Her scented love into my life?
Who's own alluring look
Draws my soul into a fusion
Of all-consuming bliss;
The gentle consummation of her kiss,
The touch of lips
And hands,
Fingers entwined
Like life itself?
Who else but she
Can understand and see
Beyond the myriad of confusions
That is me?
There is a scent about her,
So sweet that nothing can compare.
Her scent pervades and fills
The very air;
The trace of flower maidens,
Wood-sprites that you can only sense are there.
A scent I never knew before.
Awakened from lost memory,
Arising from another age,

And it binds me to her in yearning,
Touching sudden waking dreams,
Lingering brief to vanish and
Who knows what it means?
Only this; she is with me always,
And always was it seems.
Bringing Divine forgiveness
Only she, whose loveliness pervades my life
And who is she?
Oh friend, you poor unfortunate,
It is none other but
My wife.

WHO WILL SPEAK?

Who will speak up;
Will speak up for me
When I'm old?
And who will attend
When I've no more to spend
And I'm cold?
Who will come near
To give me their ear
Now I'm deaf,
Wasting their breath
To allay
My anxiety, worry and fear?
There's nobody near!
Where is the voice?
Who will consider and make
The right choice
Between Duty of Care or
Compassion and Love?

REFLECTIONS ON A LIFETIME'S LOVE
(Judy's Birthday; August 14th 2015)

What shall I write
When speaking of my Love?
Her smile? Her lips?
The sparkle from her eyes?
The tender, loving passion
That's released in perfumed sighs?

What can I write?
What words describe my Love?
Transcending any other thing
My Love's intense and pure
As from the day I met you,
And laid my Love at your door.

THE DANCE OF LOVE

The music of the Dance grows and grows,
Flowing from we two, through others whom we love,
Growing, as our love is growing, ever ceaseless, ever flowing,
Then returning, brightly burning.
And Oh! my Jude, my heart is yearning.
Love cannot be diluted, trimmed,
When love's like ours, bright and undimmed,
An endless, flowing stream like music, rising, flowing
As if a Paradisal dream.
I Love You.

WHEN YOU GO TO SLEEP
(Christmas 2015)

When you go to sleep
Then I shall come
And lay beside you
And hear again, within my head,
The laughter
That echoes through our life.
And with gentle lips
Caress you, and close my eyes,
And sleep content,
Close against you,
Close against
The softness of you.

And, when silence has replaced
The sounds of day
I shall dream,
And see you waiting
With a smile,
Oh my love,
Waiting with a smile for me.

LOVE'S JOYS RECALLED
(On Judy's birthday August 2014)

Listen! – from the innocence of childhood
Memories spring.
They cannot fade,
But live and breathe
In everything.

And from the shade
That sometimes darkens passing days
Behold! –
Love's joys recalled creep joyful,
Like a fairy from a glade.

Ah my lovely Jude –
We have a lifetime of Love
Between us.

Happy, Happy Birthday!

I AM LOOKING FOR A HEADSTONE

I'm looking for a headstone
For the 50 million dead,
But all I find are fragments
And on each of them it said,
'I remember when you were a boy
With innocence, a child,
Amusing yourself with toys before
Innocence was defiled.'

'I remember when you were a girl,
Before you were a mother;
And sweetness and love were swept away;
Bending your will to another,
Who replaced your ideals
And life's last reality
Left no room for your dreams.'

So we don't see what becomes
When dreams have been corrupted
By power and lust, and

The urge to survive were not enough
To keep you alive
And you died with your dreams
Fragmented (it seems)
Like this stone.
And in death – amongst millions –
Only we are left,
You and I,
Quite alone.

A SENSE OF NOSTALGIA

I recall the aromas of childhood,
   The sweet herbs and pitch-coated wood;
And I wander in mind
   Through the scenes left behind
When each day was happy
   And playtime was good.
The world I revisit
   Brings ease and content,
Or a smile of nostalgia
   A tear of regret
For friendship neglected,
   A sigh of relief
For mistakes unsuspected.
   The dramas of childhood
So fierce and so fraught,
   At the end of the day
Does it all count for nought?

OH JUDY
(February 2020)

It doesn't need a special time
   To say that you're my Valentine,
For when I pause and look at you
   And think of all the things you do,
The pleasure that you've brought our lives
   I know that you're the Best of Wives.
So all that I can tell you Ju,
   Is I'm so glad I married you!

THE MEETING
(January 2021)

The meeting was an accident
   The way that these things are.
I'd only seen you fleetingly
   (not 'meeting' you but 'seeing' you)
By chance the day before.
   So there you were, expecting me
To call as we'd arranged, an assignation,
   Purely chance from such a simple
Passing glance, caught as you crossed the floor.
   So here I am, nervously arriving at the door,
Shown into the living room,
   'You won't have long to wait.
She's nearly ready, won't be long.'
   The girl I'd seen the day before
Would she really like me,
   Only there to make up four?

TAUGHT BY LOVE
(February 2021)

I hear the click of the garden gate
   And hear the cluck of the hens.
And the scent of cooking in the air
   Takes me there – again.
The scuttle of moorhens in the bank
   Rustling through the rushes
While birds are perched upon the bough
   Or nesting in the bushes.
All around I hear the sounds
   Returning once again;
The baker's boy whistling on his rounds,
   The distant hoot of a train.
And I am torn
   As though re-born
To live my life again.
   But this is the life that I have loved
And this is the life I treasure,
   To live with she I call my wife,
Who has filled my life with such pleasure
   That never could I want to return,
For nothing else could measure.
   All I know – and my life will show –
That I was taught by love,
   And given love by a loving wife,
Brought from the edge of darkness
   To the light of a happy life.

* * * * * * *

Appendix

Poetry: style, form and content.

What are poems for? My answer is: to enable the reader to express feelings and emotions that might otherwise embarrass them.

We are introduced to poetry at an early age with the nursery rhymes we learn and recite; 'Hickory, dickory dock' 'Humpty Dumpty' etc. No matter their origins, they have rhythm and are melodious, pleasing and simple. Similarly the lullabies we may hear as we go to sleep also rely on an easily recognised form; a lilting melody and words that scan easily into the line. And most poetry finds its origin developing from that simple format.

Poetry has a strong relationship to music. I believe poetry and music are inextricably entwined. For even the spoken poetic word must have form; light and shade, varying degrees of emphasis and – depending on the poet's intention – an almost unconscious recognition of where the lines of verse are leading, not in the narrative sense but a musical sense, a rhythm that drives the poem along as in:

'da da - da da da - daaa…. dada, dada, dadaaa…'
'Hickory   dickory   dock,…   the mouse ran up the clock,…'

So which is the dominant imperative in poetry – the words or a sense of musical rhythm?

Perhaps the question should be, which of the two is more important to the poet?

My answer would be - neither. They ebb and flow, come and go in the poet's mind; sometimes one – melody - is the insistent theme like a metronome; at other times, in fact most times it is the words for of course it is words that drive the plot. But it is rhythm, the putting together of words that give the emphasis and shape to the unfolding plot which is so important.

Why does poetry matter? It matters because it can take the imagination of the reader on a journey; a journey into romance, into drama, it can give an insight into the metaphysical world or give expression to society's angst or dramatize an event by tapping into the emotional response of the reader in a way that prose reporting cannot.

Within this anthology of poetry are examples of different styles, tailored during the process of composing and writing to ensure there is no conflict between the underlying melody which flows from the choice and placing of the words, and the overall theme and 'feel' of the poem.

For example, one would not expect a poem on the abuse of a child to *sound* the same as a declaration of love or a poem on a pastoral theme? And yet there are similarities. Compare the opening lines from:

EVERYMAN'S CHILD
>*Where is she now, this child of mine*
>*With the innocent smile and the eyes divine?*

To;

JUDY ON A SUMMER NIGHT
>*Isn't it time that I told you again,*
>*I love you?*
>*Now that the evenings are warm and*
>*Light and the scent of the flowers fills*
>*The night, while the moth flutters up to*
>*The window light.*

And:

THE DUCHESS
>*The cutting – such a solitary place;*
>*We follow the track between the banks,*
>*Stepping along the oily sleepers,*
>*Hopping along the rustic track*
>*In the profound silence...*

In the first example the rhyming couplet is immediately presented in a compelling rhythm. But this poem is about a seriously abused child; the gentle rhyming opening lines are there to give the close a greater sense of tragedy.

Contrast with the second - 'JUDY ON A SUMMER NIGHT', a poem where the rhyming is still there but the rhyme appears at the beginning of the following line, not – as is usual – at the end.

In THE DUCHESS, a 'narrative' poem about an express train, the story begins without any opening rhymes but even without them the 'rhythm' of the poem begins to build as the narrative progresses.

What determines the form a poem should take is a combination of subject matter and content. There are no rules; a declaration of love may be the recollection of a first meeting, a shared moment, a parting. It is likely to be passionately eloquent where rhyme and alliteration conjoin to produce memorable couplets or a verse. This contrasts with a narrative story, an epic or the build-up to a memorable event, and here strict rhyming verse may be replaced by 'blank verse' where rhymes are abandoned or introduced at apparent random intervals.

Compare the opening lines of 'THE DENTIST' with the poem's closing couplet.

> *I lay in a deep, sublime, dark flowing*
> *Pool of sleep.*
> *Unconscious, unaware for all I know...*

Ending later:

> *What fearful scenes to haunt the mind.*
> *What fearful acts of men*
> *Against Mankind.*

Is it permissible to use the same lines in more than one poem? I used the same opening in two poems, one a poem with a pastoral, introspective theme MYSTIC MIST; the other THE KNIGHT OF NO RENOWN, a longer narrative romance. But I claim there is a precedent for this, although from a different artistic discipline. It is in the music of Sir Edward Elgar where we find a theme from 'The Enigma Variations' repeated twelve years later in his oratorio 'The Music Makers'. And as with Sir Edward, my two poems though sharing the same opening words, go on to address different subjects. But the opening of the verse was ideal for setting the initial tone of both poems before the subjects diverged.

Finally it must be admitted that with such a wide variety of options open to the poet in style, subject, format; where there are no 'off-limits' as to how the poet addresses his subject it can still be incredibly difficult to write a successful poem and bring it to a satisfactory conclusion. And that is why I decided to close this anthology with the 'Aftermath' which follows. These are poems that (so far) have failed.

An idea or theme suggests itself and is captured in a few choice lines that spring already formed into the mind; a rhyming couplet that sounds 'right'. But it hasn't a strong enough theme to develop and sustain it. Or a poem which is going well; the corrections are falling into place and then it inexplicably peters out and you are left with an incomplete line, struggling for the right word to give rhyme or scan. But nothing comes and the climax is somewhere far ahead from where you find yourself with no line(s) to link them and progress.

Can these unfinished verses be revived? Who knows; these poor unfinished poems are my shipwrecks strewn along a sometimes barren, rocky shore. C'est la vie!

AFTERMATH

(Aftermath: a second crop of grass in the same season)

We thought that we would change the world.
....

(unlike our forbears life's riches?)
If we did not – I ask - who did?
For now it's The army, church??

....

Are you happy with your life?
Do you know who are your friends?
Or as you view the end of life
D'you need to make amends?
Will your memory be revered?
Will it make the people pause?
Will they say in soft reflection,
That yours was a noble cause?
To live a life of peace and love;
To make another's cause your own
To emulate the Lord above
And treat the whole world as your home.

....

We aspire to be like Angels
And always tell the truth;
Be good and kind to neighbours,
And those beneath our roof.
But reality won't be denied;
Brutality's the case
When we see the real condition
Of the sorrowing human race.

War between the Nations,
War between the Faiths;
War between the Races
Our normal human state.
Bullying, suppression of
Communities at large

....

I once saw a man who hunted deer
His face was contorted in shame and fear,

....

The ones we should fear are the God-fearing good

....

What do I now embrace with Love
When Love was so much of my life?

....

Great howling, surging tossing sea,
 That climbs the cliffs and
Sprays the fields

....

THE FUTILE PURSUIT
I am resolved to reveal the greatest mystery
 By simple words, a simple truth
Beyond man's comprehension,
 Or understanding, reasoning,
Or any other faculty used to
 Justify the arrogant anxiety and doubt;
 The denial of what man cannot comprehend.

The pathetic whine, 'I can't explain...
   I need to know,'
Futile pursuit for knowledge that recedes
   And can't be understood
Through Science.
   Knowledge, that seeks to travel onward
   (Where's the End? - and when Began?)
Do you presume the mind of God?
   For only God made Pure Perfection;
'I am that I am'.
   Thus Cosmos is and will remain,
And what is worse
   The Universe
Will onward, ever onward go,
   Discovering life's imperfect flow.
Days, presaged by the wails of sorrow,
   Sun rising, keening, in the ray
Not of Sunrise, Gods great Blessing,
   Not the sun's rays on the slope
Thus rise the thoughts of early morn,
   When life and love wake with the dawn.
When day begins, when life is born.

,,,,,,,,,,,,,,,,,,,,,

Also by Brian Jackson

NOVELS

The Tears of Autumn
'Probably the best book I have read in the past four years'
(Reader M.G Amner)

Sleepers Awake
'Excellent… Why haven't we heard of this writer before?'
(Reader Ms J. Mason)

The Unacceptable Face

SHORT STORIES

Boy's Tales

FOR CHILDREN

The Butterfly Princess
(With illustrations by SAMUEL CALLAN)
'Abbi absolutely loved it…''
D Hughes (Mrs)

**Available from AMAZON and
AMAZON KINDLE**

ABOUT THE AUTHOR
Brian Jackson is a Yorkshireman, born in Sheffield. He and his wife have travelled extensively in Europe and share a love of theatre in which Brian has won awards both as actor and Director. He now lives in Herefordshire.

Made in the USA
Columbia, SC
09 April 2021

To dwell within a cave,
But each day wake afresh
And try to misbehave!'

And still life brings rewards;
(It need not bestow loneliness and fears)
Lo! See the miracle of friends
Who come to love, and with that love, respect
The steadfastness of Audrey's friendship through the years.

Life's gentle stream flows on;
Fond memory cannot tarnish or congeal
When memories new conspire to make amends
And Audrey's impish twinkle makes love real.

So let us share her laughter, see her smile,
And here today with Audrey
Enjoy each other's company awhile.

I LOVE YOU

I love you more than 'Question Time',
    I love you more than shopping.
I love you more than springtime
    Or when summer rain is dropping.
I love you when the night falls;
    I love you when it's light.
I love you in the morning
    As I've loved you through the night.
I love you when your look at me
    Makes thoughts run through my head.
I love you hidden in the woods
    And love you in our bed.
I've loved you since I met you;

Through our years of married life.
I love you Jude, for loving me,
My darling loving wife.

LIFE'S REMEMBERED LOVE
(Christmas 2014)

I recall an instant years ago;
Our two eyes shyly met;
And as sunlight melts snow on slopes
My life became renewed with hopes.

And so when our two hearts entwined
Our lives became as one;
Bound together – it cannot be denied –
Even before you were my bride.

And I have loved each moment
Of the life we two have shared.
And still I hear you gently say, 'I love you.'
Yes! – You've loved me, this I know;
You told me so each day.

And I've loved you, I hope you know
With Love such as no lady ever was before;
And pledge again, this Christmas Day,
'I love you Jude.'
My darling wife, I'll love you evermore